CLEAR

CLEAR

Carys Davies

GRANTA

Granta Publications, 12 Addison Avenue, London W11 4QR

First published in Great Britain by Granta Books, 2024

Copyright © Carys Davies, 2024

Endpaper map reproduced with the
permission of the National Library of Scotland.

A CIP catalogue record for this book
is available from the British Library.

2   4   6   8   9   7   5   3   1

ISBN 978 1 80351 040 8 (hardback)
ISBN 978 1 80351 041 5 (ebook)

Typeset in Caslon by Patty Rennie

Printed and bound by CPI Group (UK) Ltd,
Croydon, CR0 4YY

www.granta.com

for Michael

1

He wished he could swim – the swimming belt felt like a flimsy thing and it had been no comfort to be told not to worry, the men couldn't swim either.

Each time they rose he glimpsed the rocky shore, the cliffs, the absence of any kind of landing; each time they descended, the rocks vanished and were replaced by a liquid wall of grey.

He closed his eyes.

Thump.

Dear God.

He clung to the gunwale as they began to climb again and he saw, above the cliffs, a thousand birds soaring and wheeling. When the little boat tipped, and plunged into the hollow trough on the other side, he knew it would be for the last time.

But after an hour on what one of the men described later as 'an uppity sea', John Ferguson found himself safely deposited, along with his satchel and his box, on the narrow strip of sandy beach which turned out, in spite of appearances, to exist in the shadow of the monstrous cliffs.

Oh the relief of feeling solid ground beneath the soles of his soaking shoes!

Oh the relief of watching the water pour off his coat on to the hard-packed sand, and seeing in the distance – as Strachan said he would – the Baillie house, pale and almost luminous in the silvery murk of the afternoon.

With freezing fingers he unbuckled the swimming belt and tossed it cheerfully into the boat. He loosened his neckcloth and wrung it out and put it back on again. He squeezed the sea, as best he could, out of the sleeves and pockets of his coat and jumped up and down a few times in his sodden footwear in an effort to warm up. He thanked God for his deliverance.

All that remained now, before the men pushed off back across the boisterous water to the *Lily Rose*, was for one of them to carry his box while he followed with his satchel, picking his way over the rocks like a tall, slightly under-nourished wading bird, thin black hair blowing vertically in the persisting wind, silently talking to his absent wife:

'You see, Mary, it is all right. I am here. I have arrived. I am safe. You have no need to worry. I will do what I have come to do and before you know it, I will be home.'

2

The weather was calm and it rained softly.

Ivar worked hard all morning, laying new turf and straw in the places where the bad weather had torn up the roof, tying it all down with his gnarly weighted ropes. It gave him a good calm feeling to do the work – climbing up on to the roof and down again, trudging back and forth over the boggy soil and every so often pausing to sharpen his knife.

When evening came he squatted close to the fire to cook his dinner, boiling the milk for a long time until it acquired the dark colour and acrid taste he liked. When he finished eating he scraped the inside of the pot clean and wiped off the layer of soot on its underside, and after that he sat in his great chair with the cleaned pot in his lap because it was the time of year when the days are long and the nights are short and Ivar hardly ever bothered to lie down to sleep.

Outside, beyond the thick stone walls of his house, the island's contours retreated briefly into darkness but without ever really disappearing, and soon, through the opening in the roof above the hearth, light began to fall in a slowly turning, glittering column of chaff and fish scales and wisps of floating wool.

It fell on the trodden clay floor and the edge of the low table and the pot in Ivar's lap and on Ivar's sleeping face, illuminating it and separating it from the surrounding gloom the way some paintings do – a lined and weather-worn face, heavy, with a kind of hewn quality; not an old face, but not a young one either.

His hair was the colour of dirty straw, his beard darker, browner, full and perhaps unclean, with a patch of grey over his jaw on the left-hand side that stood out from the rest like a child's handprint. Having no mirror, he had no clear picture in his mind of his own appearance beyond the uncertain reflections he sometimes saw in the island's pools and puddles, though obviously he was conscious of himself in relation to his surroundings – that he was tall enough to have to stoop when he moved about inside the small, low-roofed house; that he was wide enough to fill the doorway when he ducked through it; that he was strong enough, in spite of his illness last winter, to accomplish all the tasks he needed to accomplish.

When it was fully dawn, he stepped outside.

The brook below the house had widened in the rain and everywhere the ground was sloppy. At the spring the mud lapped his feet.

He gave the old cow a drink of water and checked the knot on her tether, and then he went to find Pegi in the outfield and stayed talking to her for a while, patting her coarse and straggly mane with the flat of his hand. He called her an old cabbage and a silly, odd-looking person, and a host of other pet names he had for her in his language. In the early light her coat looked dusty and dull, a dirty-grey with a bluish-yellow tinge.

'*Prus!*' he said eventually, which was the word he used to tell her they had work to do and it was time they got going.

3

In the Baillie house, having unlocked the door and let himself in, John Ferguson emptied his satchel on to the narrow bed: his spare shirt and his second set of underwear; his comb and his soap; the blue ledger and his papers; his writing accoutrements and Mary's picture in its tooled-leather frame; the pistol, the powder, the ammunition.

It was not so snug as Strachan had led him to believe – if it had been comfortable once, it wasn't any more.

The narrow iron bed had no blanket, and the only other furniture was a low three-legged table and a single stool. He wondered if he might do better in the church, but when he walked down under a clearing sky to investigate, he found the little grey building was full of hay, and a good part of the roof had fallen in.

Well.

At least there was a cooking pot in the hearth, and on a ledge behind the house he found a small supply of peat. He also had his box, with Mary's fruit cake and his other foodstuffs inside. All of these things were blessings, and for each one he mouthed a silent prayer of thanks.

He also reminded himself that he had survived a long and horrible journey and was, praise be, no longer sea-sick. He gave thanks for that too, and as he sank down on to the little stool he reminded himself, also, that he was being paid.

So.

He would make a fire in the hearth and dry out his clothes and cook himself something to eat and try and get a good night's sleep, and in the morning he would have a little look around the island, spend the day getting his bearings, and after that he would go and find the man.

4

Ivar led Pegi down past the spring and around the base of the peaked hill. The empty baskets on her back creaked as they walked.

Steadily they plodded in the direction of the shore until they came within sight of a low-lying spit of ground below the white hill which was covered by the sea at flood tide but lay dry at the ebb.

It was dry now – a longish bank that formed a neck of land between the two low stretches of water on either side – and it was towards this slender piece of dry, rocky ground that Ivar, after leaving Pegi to graze, was walking, carrying the wooden box in which he collected and kept his bait.

There was hardly any wind, only a faint breeze towards the shore, gentle and steady against his body and his face, and for a moment he stood enjoying the sensation of the wind ruffling his hair. He'd been out very little this past spring, first because of his illness and then because of the bad weather when it had been too rough for much outdoor work, and impossible to fish off the rocks – the sea restless and unruly and wild, spindrift from the heavy breakers striking against the shore and forming a deep mist along the coast. He'd spent most of his time knitting, mainly sitting in his great chair next to the hearth but also sometimes on the stool in the byre with Pegi, occasionally talking to her but mostly just sitting in her company with a sock or a cap or whatever else he was making. Walking along the bank between the two low waters in the lightly moving wind, he thought about that, the pleasure of it – sitting with Pegi and quietly knitting; Pegi very still, his hands barely moving as they worked the needles; the only other motion a cobweb quivering in the atmosphere near the ground.

As he walked, he bent over the pools, knocking limpets off the rocks and dropping them into his bait box, and then he walked back along the beach to where Pegi was grazing and together they went round the side of the white hill and on to the tops of the cliffs, past the church where he kept his hay and along the wall that separated the burial ground from the pasture behind it. He carried on past the Baillie house and skirted the pool where his mother and his grandmother had drowned the pups, thinking he would carry on to the inlet to collect the grass for the cow's evening fodder. But he was hungry now, after the cooked milk yesterday; tired after his short night dozing in his great chair. 'You should go home, Ivar,' he told himself. 'You'll feel better after some breakfast.'

He'll remember this, of course – that he paused for a moment above the Baillie house before making up his mind whether to go home or to carry on to the inlet for the grass; he'll remember that he looked down at it and saw nothing unusual, no smoke, no open door, nothing he wouldn't have expected to see.

5

In the Baillie house John Ferguson had been unable to light a fire and unable, therefore, to dry his clothes and cook himself any dinner.

The peats on the covered ledge at the back turned out to be full of clay and refused to burn, and in the end he'd eaten a slice of Mary's fruit cake and spent a few cold and miserable hours lying in his damp clothes on the iron bed.

As soon as it was light he got up, telling himself briskly that at least he could wash himself and put a comb through his hair. According to Strachan, the nearest spring was only a short walk from the house. If the day warmed up he could spread his clothes out on the heather, and while he waited for them to dry he could perhaps begin making some preliminary notes and observations before he went to talk to the man.

The important thing was not to become dispirited – the important thing was to remember that this was a job, an errand: a means to a very important end.

He said a quick prayer and pushed his feet into his wet shoes, picked up the gun from the end of the bed and dropped it, along with the ammunition and the powder, into his box.

Everything else he returned to his satchel – his comb and his soap, his writing tin, Mary's picture and the Lowrie ledger, his spare underwear and his second shirt, which were as damp after their dash across the turbulent water from the *Lily Rose* as the ones he stood up in – and then he set off, pulling the heavy, ill-fitting door closed behind him.

The day was clear with only a low line of cloud over the horizon, and if you'd been up in the sky that morning above the island with the gannets and the guillemots, the puffins and the cormorants and the oystercatchers, you would have seen his tiny black figure leaving the Baillie house and making its way across patches of pink thrift and lush green pasture. You'd have seen it pause when it reached the first expanse of heather, and you'd have seen it remove its clothes and lay them out, along with the spare ones from inside its satchel, to dry. You'd have seen it (ivory-white now instead of black), splashing about in the reeds around the spring. You'd have seen it make a few notes in the dark-blue ledger, and then you'd have seen it get up wearing nothing but its satchel and its half-dried shoes and make its curious way over to the edge of the cliff and take a step down on to the rocky, precipitous path. You'd have seen it flailing, briefly, on the slippery stone, arms windmilling like a clumsy skater's, and when it vanished, you'd have seen its satchel arcing up and away and carried off over the water like some ungainly brown bird on an invisible current of cool northern air.

6

At the inlet, having decided against his breakfast, Ivar worked steadily, bent over and tearing armfuls of the luxuriant grass from between the rocks. Slowly he moved across them, picking the grass as he went, and it was here that he stopped and straightened himself and looked out across the water.

During his illness, dark, swimming patches had often appeared in his vision: black clots that floated before his eyes if he made the slightest movement, and for a moment he didn't move. There was a word in his language that described the covering and uncovering of a sunken rock by the sea, and it would have also described exactly the way the dark and lumpy object kept sinking beneath the shallow waves and then appearing again. He blinked, and when the dark shape was still there he dropped the grass and began to wade out, but the wind was blowing now, coming in gusts of increasing violence, and every time he reached for the lumpy mass it heaved away from him, out of reach. On the foreshore Pegi stood with her head down, the wind whipping sand against her flanks and into her eyes. Ivar snatched again at the floating object and this time he caught the edge of it and drew it close.

For a long time he stood on the beach looking out at .

the departing tide. Mist and fine rain were being driven before the wind. Sweet water trickled from the base of the cliffs behind him. He saw puffins and seals and cormorants, nothing else; for more than an hour he stood there but there was nothing and no one, no large vessel or small boat of any kind, and in the end he hung the satchel from his shoulder, packed the grass into Pegi's baskets, turned his back on the beach and went home.

In the satchel he found a bundle of sodden papers inside a blue cloth cover; a comb like the one Hanus had once brought back for Jenny from Bergen, the time he got the tea and the tobacco, only smaller and with smoother teeth; a piece of corn-coloured soap, soft and squashy from all the water; a tin containing a small folding knife and what he believed to be writing implements; and right at the bottom, under the papers, he found a dark-haired woman inside a leather frame, looking up at him from behind a piece of broken glass with a shy and secret smile.

It was impossible to make out her surroundings, which were misty and brown and indistinct, as if she was standing in the grainy gloaming of an early winter afternoon. But the woman herself was as alive as anything he'd ever seen, and more alive, by far, than his memories of Jenny or his mother or his grandmother. In his whole life he had never seen anything like her. He touched her with his finger, almost expecting her to move, and for a long time he knelt before the fire holding her.

It was late when he stood up and propped her against the wall on the stone shelf above the hearth while he separated the soaking papers that were in the bag and spread them out in front of the fire to dry. If there'd been anything written on them, any words in English or Scots or Danish or Norwegian or any other language he didn't know and couldn't read, they had been washed away. The blue cloth they'd been wrapped in he wrung out with his hands and spread that out too. The soap he lifted to his face but it smelled of nothing but the sea and he set it down on the hearth next to the comb and then, even though everything was already illuminated by the fire, he lit the lamp so he could look again at the smiling dark-haired woman who was somehow alive inside the frame and the murky brown darkness that surrounded her.

7

The picture of Mary Ferguson in the tooled-leather frame was a calotype by Robert Adamson.

It was made in Edinburgh a few months after the Fergusons' marriage, and six weeks after the Reverend John Ferguson resigned his living in the city's northern parish of Broughton and became a poor man by throwing in his lot with the Free Church of Scotland.

'Me? Oh no, John. Not a picture! Not of me. Please no!'

But John Ferguson was too excited to be put off. 'Not a *picture*, Mary. A calotype. A way of seizing and preserving a living image – from the Greek, from *kalos*, meaning beautiful.'

John already had an appointment of his own with Adamson – the young photographer who had embarked upon the task of bringing as many of the rebellious ministers of the new Free Church as would come to his Rock House studio at the foot of Calton Hill. Working from the calotypes, his friend, the artist David Octavius Hill, would then paint them on to a vast canvas commemorating this historic split between the established Church and the new one.

Mary was nervous before the camera, and acutely conscious of her teeth. (It is perhaps why she looks so shy in the resulting image, and not as forceful as she could be in real life.) She also found the image a little ghostly in spite of its magical reality. She could see it was her own living self that the young Mr Adamson had somehow seized and frozen with his liquids and his light – that it was undoubtedly her, standing on the sheltered, foggy-looking back lawn behind his studio, and yet it gave her the unsettling feeling that she was looking at a picture of herself after she'd died; that it was some sort of memorial, or souvenir.

John, though, was enchanted.

Solemn, even severe, in repose, his bony Presbyterian face broke into a delighted smile when they returned to collect it, and he saw for the first time what had been achieved. With effusive thanks to Mr Adamson, he took Mary into the first small shop they came to at the foot of Calton Hill and spent what must have been almost the last of his money on a rectangular leather frame. With the calotype safely behind the glass, he slipped it into his satchel, kissed his new wife's hand and said, 'There. Now if we are ever separated, I will still have you with me, my most precious darling, at all times.'

8

If a vessel had come and gone, Ivar hadn't seen it.

If a vessel had come and been sunk by the storm, he hadn't seen that either, nor any small boat digging its way fiercely to shore. He'd stayed inside all day and all night and hadn't stepped out until he knew the wind had died and he was ready to begin working on the roof.

He went down now to the beach to look for any bits and pieces that might have come from a wreck, but there was nothing. From the top of the white hill he looked out in every direction, scanning the water for the remains of a vessel or a boat or anything drifting, but there was nothing he could see from there either, only the pasture and the cliffs and the choppy wash of the waves near the beach, the swell further out. As the waves gathered towards the shore they resembled veins raised beneath the skin of the sea, moving in a shifting line that altered and broke like a line of geese heading north, but they brought nothing with them. He closed his eyes and opened his mouth to hear better, but there was nothing then either – nothing he wouldn't have expected to hear.

When he went out again, later, he took the woman with him in the big pocket of his short wool coat.

He took her with him when he went to fetch water from the spring and when he went fishing off the rocks. He took her with him when he went to collect limpets and when he went to pick spurrey from between the potatoes to give to the old black cow to eat, and when he went to the round hill to bring home the peats.

When he cooked his dinner he propped her against the wall on the stone shelf above the fire, and when he went to sleep in his great chair he tucked her inside his jumper between his collarbone and his heart.

9

My brother-in-law's circumstances are very narrow since he renounced his emoluments, Andrew Armstrong had written to his godfather, Henry Lowrie.

It was likely to be a temporary situation, he'd explained, one which would last only until the new Free Church progressed towards the building of its own churches and generally poured its stubborn principles and evangelical energies into new livings for its impoverished ministers, of which his brother-in-law was one.

His name is John Ferguson, he'd written, *and although he is a churchman, I can vouch for his ability to make himself generally useful, his father having been a steward on a large estate across the water in Fermanagh.*

What Henry Lowrie thought of John Ferguson's break with the established Church is not recorded; if he was irked by the new Free Church's revolt against the right of landowners like himself to confer clerical livings on ministers of their choice (or, to put it another way, distribute favours according to their own wishes), he didn't say so.

What seems likely is that, in his opinion, one Presbyterian minister was much the same as another – none of them, in his experience, having kicked up any sort of fuss about the removal of people from estates like his own in order for them to be replaced by sheep. Whether they'd stayed with the established Church or come out with the new one, it made no difference; they had not interfered.

Indeed, the Presbyterian doctrine of providence had proved something of a boon in clearing the people – reminding them, as it did, that the events of their lives were no more than the unfolding of God's will; that any suffering accruing from their removal was no more than divine punishment for their sins. All of it nonsense in Henry Lowrie's opinion, but if that was what the Church believed and chose to preach, so be it, and all the better as far as he was concerned.

It seems likely, then, that it didn't take long for Henry Lowrie to mull over his godson's proposal before deciding that having a clergyman help out on his estate might be unusual, but was in no way unattractive, and he wrote back by return of post, saying he'd be happy for Reverend Ferguson to travel up to Perth and meet his factor, who was very busy at the present time and could quite possibly benefit from a little assistance.

The Lowries had been relatively slow to begin the time-consuming process of clearing their land, partly because Henry's son, James, had an entrepreneurial streak and had been pestering his father to consider various experimental ventures south of the border – a salt mine and a copper-smelting house in Liverpool; a manufactory of mohair and twist buttons in Macclesfield; an opportunity in gypsum in Derbyshire; a place outside Stafford where there was earthenware to be profitably made.

But to each new scheme Henry Lowrie's response had

been the same: the estate had no cash, no money at all; nowhere were the rents keeping pace with expenditure, and in the end even James had been convinced by the example of other landowners who had simply decided to replace people with sheep, and in doing so were making the best of what they already had.

James had soon become as enthusiastic as his father about taking the same big broom that others had been busy with all over Scotland, from Lanark in the south to Sutherland in the north, and it was galling to him now that they were so behindhand with their own removals when others – first in the Lowlands and then in the Highlands – had been making improvements, sweeping clean the countryside for decades and reaping the rewards. Like his father, he'd become impatient to make up for lost time – for there to be more and more portions of the Lowrie estate that were rented out to a single flockmaster – where you could stand on a hill or rise and look out over clean, productive country that was quietly replete with sheep, instead of cluttered with the ramshackle dwellings of small, impoverished, unreliable tenants scraping a profitless living in a manner that no longer made any sense.

John and Mary Ferguson arrived early on a Saturday morning with the mail coach from Edinburgh and went straight to the estate office.

They stood while Strachan, the Lowrie factor, bent over a map laid out on the table between them, tapped his finger on a spot a great distance from the coast, and told them without preamble that the proposal in this particular case was for upwards of a thousand sheep.

Reverend Ferguson, he said, was to carry out a survey of this out-of-the-way corner of the estate to assess the adequacy and extent of the pasture and whether there had been any deterioration or significant change in the years since he, Strachan, had stopped calling there for the rent. 'You should bear in mind, Reverend, how good the sheep will be at making the most of every inch of available grazing – how nimble they will be, and as happy to browse the shore as the tops of the hills. Far better, say, than a pack of black Highland cattle when it comes to ferreting nourishment from the most inaccessible places between the rocks, and not averse to a little seaweed to supplement their diet.' The stout factor paused to execute a wink and a brief, dry smile in the direction of his new helper: 'Also much less likely than a crowd of large, slow-moving cattle to go tumbling off the edges of the cliffs into the sea.'

The new Lowrie sheep would be purchased in the Northern Isles and brought across – compact, resilient little animals with long legs and a fine fleece. There would be no need for anyone to live on the island; a few shepherds and a gang of boys and dogs would visit three times a year – once in November to put on the tups, once in the summer to bring off the wool, and once in the autumn to pick up the lambs. Other than that, the excellent creatures would look after themselves.

Mary knew next to nothing about the management of sheep, but it seemed to her it would be helpful to have someone on the island whose familiarity with its nooks and crannies, its high places and its clefts, would be far better than any stranger's. 'And the man who John is to remove – could he not stay and do the shepherding?'

As soon as the words were out of her mouth she'd glanced at John, conscious that she had said something unhelpful; if the man stayed, John would not be sent to remove him, and would not be paid.

Strachan looked at his feet, and when he spoke to Mary it was in a slow, patient, almost fatherly voice, as if he were addressing a stupid child. 'No, he could not, Mrs Ferguson. As I said, there is no requirement for anyone, any more, to be there all year round. Any inhabitant such as this one is quite redundant and, with his own needs and the needs of his motley collection of livestock, an encumbrance.'

Perhaps the Lowrie factor thought Mary was having trouble grasping what he was telling her because he rephrased it then, in a slightly different way: 'We can't have squatters on any of our land who take, Mrs Ferguson, but cannot afford to give – neither now, nor at any time in the future. If the island is ever sold, or the tenancy transferred, it will want to be sold, or leased, clean. He will be brought to a substantially more comfortable place on the coast where he will be able to turn his hand to forestry, or sea fishing, and will I'm sure do very well for himself.'

Mary stood, thinking of the reports she'd read in the newspapers over the years of people in Sutherland and Wester Ross and the Hebrides who had not, in fact, done well for themselves; who had wanted very much to stay where they were and farm, instead of seeing their houses burned or reduced to rubble and the land they'd worked for generations laid under sheep.

She looked at John. They'd gone over it all many times since Andrew had shown them Henry Lowrie's letter outlining the nature of the work the estate factor, Mr

Strachan, was currently undertaking, and the particular errand in which Reverend Ferguson could be of immediate assistance.

'So will John be bringing the man's livestock away too?'

Strachan paused. He was tired of Mary Ferguson's questions, and turned to her husband to answer this one.

'No, he won't.'

As far as he recalled, there were some chickens and a small bevy of scrawny indigenous sheep, a blind cow that was good for nothing apart from being spoon-fed huge quantities of the best grass on the island, and a bad-tempered horse with a ridiculous name he couldn't remember.

'Keane will dispose of them all when he returns in a month's time to fetch you off, Reverend, and I've no doubt he'll pay our man fairly, when he leaves, for the loss of his magnificent beasts.'

10

Pale and shining in the cool sunlight, from a distance the naked man resembled an enormous jellyfish.

Pegi saw him first, and stopped without Ivar expecting her to, so that he stumbled against her before they came to a halt.

He bent down.

The man lay with his arms outstretched and his face to the sky. On one foot he wore a single shoe. He was terribly bruised and cut all over and Ivar could see a few small stones in his open mouth, which made him think he must be dead, but when he touched his cheek he felt his breath against his wrist.

He stood up, looked out across the water and closed his eyes, his ears full of the cries of curious and hungry gulls trembling on invisible currents overhead; of the wallop of the waves, and the noisy scrabble of the beach being dragged out beneath them as they retreated.

In the pocket of his short coat his hand closed round the leather frame, gripping it tightly, because he was not such a fool that he didn't understand it belonged to this naked stranger.

He would have struggled to put his feelings into words, but it's fair to say that in less than two short days the woman inside the frame had become precious to him, and he would have preferred it if the man had been dead.

He leaned against Pegi, and for a long time he hesitated.

He wished the old horse would speak and tell him what to do, but she didn't, and eventually he removed the big wicker baskets from her back and set them down in the sand, and when a battered black coat came tumbling towards them like a snarl of ragged seaweed, he took hold of it by one of its tattered sleeves and stooped, and lifted the man in his arms, and settled him across Pegi's back in the baskets' place with the coat covering him, and when his weight was equally balanced, with his head hanging down on one side and his feet on the other, the three of them proceeded slowly along the beach below the precipitous path in the cliff from which the Reverend John Ferguson, losing his footing in his thin-soled shoes, had fallen.

11

Ivar rolled him in a knitted shawl.

He scraped the hard deposits of blood and sand from the big oblong wound in the back of his head and washed the lesser scrapes and cuts on his narrow face and hands. His left leg was swollen from what Ivar reckoned was a break above the ankle and he wound this tightly with a piece of his prickly home-made rope, thinking, as he took hold of the bones, 'This will be the moment when he cries out in pain,' but he didn't. John Ferguson didn't cry out and he didn't wake up.

Ivar sat in his great chair and at some point he must have slept, because when he woke light was falling through the square opening in the roof above the hearth. On his bed the man lay sleeping or unconscious, he didn't know which.

He rose stiffly, ground a little corn, stirred it into yesterday's leftover milk and put it on the fire to warm, but even with all this clatter and moving about the man still didn't wake up or alter his position in any way.

It had happened once, when Ivar was a boy – one of the men had fallen from the fowling cliff and wasn't killed, but he'd never opened his eyes or moved again, except that sometimes his eyelids would jump, and in the small crack between the upper and lower lids you'd see his eyeballs, only they never moved in the way a sleeping person's did, they just lay there like white pebbles. For a month there was no change, no movement apart from the occasional twitching of the eyelids, which was enough to sustain his wife in her belief that he was perpetually on the brink of waking up, but he never did, and eventually, he died.

Ivar leaned forward in his great chair and peered at the man's face in the firelight. His eyelids did not flutter; there was no crack between them, and Ivar couldn't see if behind the thin and wrinkled skin his eyes were moving like a sleeping person's, or lying there like white pebbles.

Towards evening he had a smoke, pinching out a few of the remaining threads of tobacco that were still left from when the Norwegians had come. The tobacco was old now and stale, with no more flavour than if he'd stuffed his pipe with a bit of ground-up sheepskin, but still, he liked the feeling of the smoke being pulled down inside his body and then watching it leave him in a rough torrent that collapsed into a flattened, stringy cloud, like a skein of yarn that slowly disintegrated and became absorbed into the atmosphere around him.

He took out the woman from inside his sweater and ran his thumb across her mouth. He didn't know what to do.

12

Mary never wanted it to be John who went, but Strachan said he had his hands full elsewhere.

She'd listened while the squat, red-faced factor told John that he would have no trouble; that there was no one left now on the island but the idiot son, the one who hadn't drowned, and he – assuming he was still there – was as placid and obedient as an old heifer.

'How will I convey the decision to him?' said John, and Strachan said he would give him a document that explained the terms of his eviction. Unfortunately, the old Shetlander he used to take up there as an interpreter when he went for the rent was dead now, and there was no one left, as far as he knew, who spoke the island's peculiar tongue. But the *Lily Rose* would be stopping off on Orkney, where Reverend Ferguson could visit the Kirkwall schoolteacher if he fancied equipping himself with a handful of useful words and phrases with which to distil his message. The schoolteacher was familiar with the old vernacular and would help him compose a short speech. 'You can put yourself together a little dictionary, Reverend.'

Then from a cabinet on the wall Strachan had produced a pistol.

John took a step backwards and his mouth opened, but

before any words came out the Lowrie factor had placed the weapon in his hands.

'I thought you said he was placid and obedient.' Mary spoke more sharply than she'd meant to, but she couldn't help it.

'And so he is, Mrs Ferguson.' Strachan scratched the small, sickle-shaped scar next to his mouth. 'Very placid and very obedient.'

The Lowrie factor had an easy, confident way about him, and the broad smile he directed at Mary was both confident and easy. 'He is, however, very large and very accustomed to being where he is, and I wouldn't want to send the Reverend off without something to fall back on in the unlikely event that our man becomes excitable.' And besides, he added, no one would want to have to rely solely on his box of Lowrie provisions during his stay – a few fresh tasty birds, of which there would be a greater abundance than he had ever seen in his life, would liven things up nicely and the pistol was just the job for that.

It was a big, unwieldy-looking instrument, and Mary watched John's long unpractised fingers fumble with its moving parts while Strachan delivered a brisk lesson in its operation.

She wanted to say that John would never, in any circumstances, pick up a weapon to resolve a disagreement with another human being; instead, she took a breath and counted to three. She hated that they were beholden – hated John having to jump when Strachan said 'jump' – but with Strachan bent over the gun, John was discreetly looking at her and telling her with his eyes that it was best if she left it there, and later that evening he put on a big

show of being cheerful, saying that if St Paul could earn
his crust for a while in Corinth as a tent-maker, then surely
an impoverished minister of the Free Church of Scotland
could put his shoulder to a little temporary factoring.

Even so, they were both anxious on the evening of John's
departure from Aberdeen.

Neither of them spoke as they walked along the quay
towards the *Lily Rose*, and both tried not to listen to the
noisy crackle in John's pocket of the official Summons of
Removing.

At supper the previous evening, Mary's brother-in-law
Andrew (who happened to be passing through Perth –
the same Andrew who'd written to his godfather Henry
Lowrie on John's behalf, asking for the favour of a little
paid employment) had expressed the opinion that when
John delivered his message, the man would receive it like
the answer to a prayer, such was the squalor and difficulty
of the hardscrabble lives lived in places as remote and des-
olate as his. 'He will be much better served,' said Andrew,
'in his new location.'

Mary said she hoped so, and afterwards, in bed, John
said that no doubt there were many places in the countryside where Andrew's assessment was correct.

Mary lay quietly, and after a short silence said she
thought that was almost certainly the case, even if there
were others where it wasn't – where people had been
cleared from their homes to some meagre, infertile spot
or sent to fish on some tempestuous stretch of coast where
there were no harbours, or carted off in disease-ridden
ships to the other side of the world.

Into her mind a picture came of this vast emptying-out – a long, grey and never-ending procession of tiny figures snaking their way like a river through the country. She saw them moving away with quiet resignation, leading animals and small children, carrying tools and furniture and differently sized bundles, and when at last they disappeared she saw the low houses they'd left behind, roofless hearths open to the rain and the wind and the ghosts of the departed while sheep nosed between the stonework, quietly grazing. She remembered a dinner, a long time ago now, at her father's house in Penicuik, where the talk had turned to a removal somewhere north of Cannich, and remembered her father remarking that he was surprised there was still anyone left to remove – that he thought all the big estates must by now have been thoroughly cleansed of their unwanted people.

She waited for John to say something about providence but he didn't. For a long moment neither of them spoke, until eventually John said, 'Strachan says our man is sure to flourish once he turns his hand to forestry.'

After that there was a longer silence during which each supposed the other had gone to sleep. But in the early hours Mary heard John say, 'The money is a significant amount,' and Mary said, yes it was.

She knew how worried he was about money.

In the months before he put his name to the Deed of Demission, separating the new Free Church from the established one, he'd been away from home for most of every week, dashing around Edinburgh and travelling to Glasgow and Stirling and Aberdeen, attending meetings and paying calls, and as far as she could tell an enormous amount of time and energy had been taken up with the question of how the new Church would finance itself.

His letters home had been full of forecasts and estimates – how much the Church could expect in contributions from its congregations, how much in gifts and regular subscriptions. There was to be a central fund for the building of churches and schools, and a separate one to provide its ministers with an adequate stipend. Richer parishes would help the poorer ones, and in time, it was hoped, every minister would receive £150 annually. 'But I struggle to see,' he'd written, 'how in Broughton – even if the entire congregation comes out with me, as I believe it will – we will muster more than £35 in contributions towards a stipend in the first year.' He'd begun ending his letters with an account of all the money he'd spent while he'd been away from her: six shillings for the coach from Glasgow; three shillings on dinner; two and six on lunch; twopence on postage etc. He cancelled his subscription to the *Scottish Guardian* (two shillings), and although he'd never cut down on how often he wrote to her (daily), he'd begun reducing by half the amount of paper he used, his writing so cramped and minuscule she could hardly read it without a magnifying glass.

He worried about everything. He worried about raising enough money to buy a stove to keep the congregation warm this coming winter in whatever temporary structure they might be able to find to serve as their church. He worried about being able to spare a pound, annually, to pay a reliable person to watch the stove and stand at the doors to greet people when they came in and welcome them and be polite to them. He worried he wouldn't have enough money to buy folding chairs for people to sit on, let alone a set of Communion vessels or a pulpit robe for himself. He fretted about ever being able to afford £10 a year for a precentor to lead the singing, and even though pledges were starting to come in, he worried that it would be years before they could think of building a permanent church with pews and pew doors: something dignified and solid and enduring with a clock and a bell and coloured windows and a font; a steeple of iron and stone.

But most of all, she knew, he worried about her; about where they would live and what sort of home he would be able to provide, how he would put food on the table and coal in the grate. He was obsessed with the predicament of his friend, Dr Tullock, who after moving out of the manse at Carmyllie, near Arbroath, was living in a turf hut on the banks of the River Tay, while his family lodged in the cabin of an abandoned boat where on Sundays, in the open air, he preached from the deck. Mary had told him repeatedly that she could think of many worse things than living in an old boat, but he only nodded, and she knew what he was thinking: that he was failing her as a husband; that he was sacrificing her comfort and security at the altar of his principles and his faith.

They'd had the same conversation so many times in the course of the past few months – Mary telling him it didn't matter and she didn't care, and John saying it *did* matter and *he* cared. He hardly slept any more, and at the table he pushed his food around his plate without eating it. He wrote to friends, and friends of friends, asking if they were in need of a temporary tutor for their children; he wrote to his friend Adam Grant, asking if the Medical School needed someone to help with the translating of its anatomy catalogues from Latin into English so that they could be perused by tourists.

And then a few weeks ago she'd thought he seemed more at ease – finally less fretful – only to discover that he'd asked Andrew if Andrew might be able to help him procure some paid employment; only to find that Andrew had written to Henry Lowrie, and that John had asked another minister in the new Free Church to please look after the people in his Broughton congregation who had come out with him; to please preach to them, and pray with them in the open air while he was away in the north.

For a whole day she'd refused to speak to him.

'Mary,' he'd said, as they prepared for bed, 'please don't be angry.'

'I'm not angry, John,' she'd said. 'Just surprised.' She knew how worried he was, she said, about money, of course she did, but it did surprise her that he would involve himself with someone like Lowrie. 'After everything you've been through over the patronage question. Everything you've stood up for. That you'd go trotting off like this to do his bidding.'

She knew what he was going to say before he said it: that this had nothing to do with the patronage question; that surveying a small island and seeing to the transfer of its last remaining inhabitant to a new and more suitable location was a purely economic errand; that it had nothing to do with rich men doling out clerical livings and generally meddling with the spiritual independence of the

Church; that the land was Lowrie's and he had every right to organise it as he saw fit.

Now, as they walked along the quay towards the *Lily Rose*, Mary was silent, and although she was still unhappy that he'd decided to go, she regretted accusing him of 'trotting off'. She also regretted calling him pompous, which at some point she'd done because she was so cross and frustrated, and the truth was that John was not pompous. He was the least overbearing, most sincere person she'd ever met.

They'd both been quiet on the long road from Perth to Aberdeen, though once in a while John had talked again about the money, and how it would be calculated at a rate of fivepence a mile, and how there was a large benefit, therefore, in the place being so remote and faraway.

'By the time I reach Lerwick I will have earned seven pounds!' he'd announced enthusiastically as they rattled through Stonehaven, and even though the rate would be reduced by half from Lerwick onwards, if everything went well, at the end of it all he'd be bringing home the very substantial sum of nearly sixteen pounds, for them and for the new Church, from this one simple expedition.

Mary nodded.

Well, all right.

She knew John's savings amounted to no more than nine pounds; she wasn't going to say that another sixteen wouldn't be helpful.

Nor was she going to say that things might have been easier if he'd been willing to accept Andrew's earlier offer to lend them some money, instead of him going halfway to Norway to earn it. Nor was she going to tell him again that it surprised her he was prepared to accept work from a landowner like Henry Lowrie, because she knew what he'd say, and then they'd have the same argument all over again about the separation of the worldly and the spiritual, and there'd be a good chance he'd end up bringing the Gospels into it with his '*Render unto Caesar the things that are Caesar's, and unto God the things that are God's.*' And even though he would apologise afterwards for quoting scripture at her because he knew how much it irritated her, the peace between them would feel fragile, and that was the last thing she wanted when they were about to be separated from each other for a whole entire month.

At the quayside she reached up and folded down his coat collar, which was sticking up, and smoothed it and patted it like a mother who was sending her only son off into the navy and was determined not to disgrace herself by crying.

'Off you go then, John Ferguson,' she said.

13

Morning came. The stars faded away.

Ivar went around the outfield picking up stones to add to the heap on top of the rotting coalfish. He sorted his potatoes into two piles, big ones and little ones. He spent half an hour tying rags on the feet of the hens to stop them scratching up the seed corn.

Inside, he stirred a little meal into a pan of milk and boiled it, but when he sat down in his great chair with the pan he found he couldn't eat it.

He tried to knit but he couldn't settle, and when he sat down at his spinning wheel it was the same – the yarn kept snapping and he couldn't relax.

He took the woman out from under his jumper. She was older than Jenny but younger, he thought, than his mother. He drew his finger along the outline of her sleeves until he reached her elbows, then past them on to the remainder of her arms all the way to her hands which were lost in the puffy lap of her enormous skirt.

He thought about hiding her in the wooden box – not the one where he kept his bait but the other, bigger one, where he kept his meal – but the minute she was in there with the lid closed he missed having her with him and took her out and pushed her back under his jumper.

He picked up the man's comb, the bar of soap, the big satchel itself which was stiff and dry and marked all over with wavy, crumbling lines of salt. In his great chair he sat with them for a while in his lap and then he put them down again on the hearth and took hold of the man's metal tin.

The little knife inside it opened like a shell: two halves that resisted slightly when he pushed them apart with his fingers but remained firmly joined together at a point in the middle.

He tested the blade against his thumb and stepped over to the bed and to the man, who seemed peaceful. He wondered if he might choose this moment to wake up, but when he put his hand under the heavy head nothing happened, the man's eyes stayed closed and his breathing went on peacefully and evenly as before. Ivar pushed his hand further under the head so he could get a little more purchase on it, and then he tilted it and began cutting away the hair around the big wound.

In some places it was so hard-packed and stuck-together he had to loosen it first with his fingers because he couldn't see where it started and where it finished. It was as if it had begun to put down new roots into the wound itself, and it made a tearing sound as he cut, reminding him of the sound his sheep made pulling at the grass with their teeth, or of his own pulling at the reeds that continually encroached around the spring, choking it. There. That was better. He threw the dark cut-away hair on to the fire where it sizzled and burned away to nothing, and then he peered curiously at what his cutting had revealed, which was a circle of clear white bone that seemed to be neither cracked nor chipped but left him no wiser than before as to whether the man would recover or not.

In the dim firelight he examined the narrow face. Blue-grey and still, it had a sharp nose and dark eyebrows that were higher at the sides than where they met in the middle – like a bird, flying. Ivar peeled back the knitted blanket. The hands lay with their palms upwards, their fingers curled, the tips scorched – raw. The knees were also skinned, and a large part of the chest over the ribcage, both hips. He must have fallen with a burning speed.

Suddenly a horrible, wet, gritty, gargling sound came bubbling up out of the man's throat – as if the little stones that had been in his mouth when he was lying on the beach were still in there, and Ivar wondered if what he was hearing was the noisy, rattling breath of someone who was about to die. But the gargling sound stopped as suddenly as it had started, and the man's breath came quietly, a dulcet in-and-out whisper punctuated every now and then with a tiny sighing squeak, and about an hour after that, he opened his eyes.

14

Slowly John Ferguson looked around at the walls and up at the opening in the roof, blinking once, twice, and then a third time before his eyes came at last to rest on Ivar himself.

He tilted his head slightly, but then he grimaced, and drew in his breath sharply, and was still again.

In a rusty, rasping voice he spoke a few words of what Ivar thought was English or Scots or a mixture of the two.

'Ivar,' said Ivar in a slow, reluctant way, placing the palm of his big hand heavily on the front of his thick and filthy sweater.

'John Ferguson,' whispered John Ferguson before his eyes closed again.

15

He couldn't think where he was or what had happened to him.

His eyelids were so heavy that every few seconds he had to close them again. The rest of the time he wasn't always asleep, but he was so dazed, and the pain in his chest and behind his eyes and in his leg was so ferocious if he shifted his position even a little, that all he could do was lie on his back without moving. When he did open his eyes he could see a clay jug he didn't recognise and there was a foul odour everywhere of fish and decay. He saw a spinning wheel and a blue and white teapot and a chair with a tall wicker back and sides, a cooking pan and a mound of dirty wool, all of it unknown to him.

He remembered standing on the quay with Mary and he thought he'd been at sea, but for how long, or where he'd been going, he couldn't say. The only thing he felt sure of was the feeling that he was not surprised to see the big fair-haired man looming over him; that there was something important about him he was supposed to know, but whatever it was lay just beyond his grasp – some detail which, like the reason he'd been at the quayside with Mary, and what had happened to him since he left her, he had forgotten.

*

It was peaceful, watching the slight movements of the big needles in the man's hands while he knitted, and when he was spinning to follow the passage of the thread as it was twisted and guided by the fly to the spool. The spinning wheel made him think of fairy tales and being a boy in Dundee at the house on Balfour Street. The telling of fairy tales had been forbidden by his aunt, but her housekeeper, Annie, had told them to him anyway, and it was far from unpleasant, lying motionless, floating in and out of sleep or unconsciousness, watching the knitting and the spinning.

Things were uncomfortable for Ivar, though, now that the man was awake for brief periods during the day.

He was conscious all the time of having the woman hidden inside his jumper, and there were moments when he had the feeling the man must know she was there.

He resented not being able to take her out any more whenever he wanted to. Even when the man, John Ferguson, had his eyes closed and seemed to have fallen again into one of his deep sleeps, he couldn't shake off the suspicion that the stranger was watching him from behind his closed eyes, and although Ivar hated how furtive it made him feel, when he wanted to be alone now with the woman, he took her outside.

16

John Ferguson remembered wishing he could swim.

He remembered thinking that the swimming belt felt like a flimsy thing. He remembered the rocks and the liquid wall of grey and making his way through a meadow of pink thrift.

He thought of the way the different coloured threads in Mary's work basket lay coiled, partly touching and partly not. That was how he felt: that some of the threads of himself were connected but most of them weren't, and that he was continually on the point of joining them all together without ever managing it. It was like searching for a word he knew but couldn't pluck from his brain.

He lay with his eyes slightly open, and in the gloomy daylight he surveyed the bare, thick walls of the hovel. His weary gaze moved along the runnel of dirty water in the clay floor beside his bed that seemed to drain out through a gap between two stones in the corner. Over and over his eyes travelled across the iron cooking pot and the large wicker chair and the big fair-haired man sitting in it, and upwards to the high shelf over the door with the incongruously beautiful blue and white teapot sitting on it, and from there to a long black coat suspended from a peg in the wall which, after looking at it for a long time, he recognised as his own, freakishly altered by the addition of a pair of pale-red knitted sleeves.

Where were the rest of his clothes? He knew he wasn't wearing them; he could feel the scratchy wool of the blanket on top of his skin, all the way from his neck to his feet.

On the hearth he could see his satchel and one of his shoes and a heap of papers he thought must be his Gospels, the sheets lying one on top of the other, crisp and undulating, like a pile of autumn leaves. But he couldn't see Mary. Perhaps she was in the bag? He hoped so, because he felt bereft without her, and the stiff, salt-stained bag looked, like his Gospels, as if it had been in the water, and he couldn't get out of his mind a picture of her beautiful portrait rolling across the lumpy floor of the ocean among the weeds and the fishes, as if Mary herself were being tossed about and drowned. He tried to lift his hand to point to the satchel but it was too painful and he was too exhausted, his vision had turned cloudy, and when he tried to ask the man to pass it to him he was too tired to say the words, and a moment later he was sleeping again.

What, if he'd been looking on, would John Ferguson's old university friend, Adam Grant, have said?

Grant, who regularly peered into the open heads of cadavers on the dissecting table at the anatomy theatre on South Bridge in Edinburgh; Grant, who had talked to John Ferguson for hours on end about the mysteries of the human brain when they were both students hurrying up and down the narrow streets and steps of the Old Town, noisily discussing medicine and theology.

Well, for a start, being a great reader, he would probably have complained about the fashion beloved by the worst kind of contemporary novelists for inflicting catastrophic and prolonged memory loss on their characters – very likely he would have called it a cheap plot device to complicate an already complicated series of events.

No doubt he would have poured scorn, too, on the popular myth that the best way to restore a misplaced memory after being hit once on the head was to be hit again.

Almost certainly, he would have told his friend John Ferguson not to worry – that his brain was probably just a little swollen, and that in cases like his, amnesia rarely extends beyond a few hours or at most a few days, during which it is quite normal to experience a certain amount of confusion and bewilderment.

Which is exactly what happened to John Ferguson: all the disconnected threads of himself coming together in a rush when he woke up on the morning of the fourth day. With sparkling clarity he remembered exactly where he was and why he'd come and what it was he needed to do now that he was here. The knowledge blew through him like a blast of cold, invigorating air, leaving him wide awake and wondering how best to proceed.

17

He'd found the Orkney schoolteacher easily enough in a tall yellow house with a black door at the top of Albert Street, just south of Kirkwall harbour.

But it turned out Strachan had oversold William Flett's ability to help; when John Ferguson named his destination, Flett said there was no one alive any more, as far as he knew, who spoke the island's ancient language. His own dialect bore a slight resemblance here and there but it was not the same.

'Oh,' said John Ferguson glumly, which was rude of him, but he had been ill from the moment the *Lily Rose* left Aberdeen. He was a poor sailor at the best of times, anxious and fearful of the water, and his unremitting nausea had left him very tired. On top of which he'd become increasingly worried, lying in his foetid bunk, that when he found the man and explained to him what was to happen, he would fail to do it properly, that he would be unable to describe to him the advantages of his new location, or explain to him, if he seemed reluctant to accept the news calmly, that God's purpose lies behind everything in our lives, even if we cannot at first see it. He worried that things would go badly, and he would have to resort to making threats with a weapon he scarcely knew how to use.

'I'm sorry,' said Flett. 'You're disappointed, Reverend.'

'No, no, no. Forgive me. I mean, yes I am, a little, I suppose. I was hoping to be able to give him the news in words that would be familiar to him.'

Flett, who was even taller and thinner than John Ferguson, and had a dry sense of humour, said he understood; delivering unexpected news was tricky at the best of times and it was always good to remember that when the Armenian king, Tigranes, was told to prepare for the arrival of General Lucius Licinius Lucullus and his Roman hordes, he had the messenger's head cut off. Still, said Flett brightly, he would be happy to write out a short speech in his own dialect, because there was a goodish chance the man John Ferguson was going to visit would grasp its general drift and understand the positive aspects of what he was being told. 'I will keep it simple for you, Reverend, and give you some guidance as to the behaviour of its vowels and its consonants and its general pronunciation.'

18

The speech was gone.

When John Ferguson gestured weakly to Ivar to pass him the pile of crispy, leaf-like papers on the hearth, he saw at once that they were empty. He turned them over with his scuffed-up fingertips and when there were no more to turn over he said, 'Oh dear.'

Because the Summons of Removing was gone too, its copperplate wording dissolved and washed away by the water.

Also gone was his translation of the Gospels – what Mary called, with affectionate patience, his 'Great Project' – which he now wished he'd left at home but hadn't, because you never knew when the right word or phrase would come to you, and there was always a risk that it wouldn't come to you again in the same way if you didn't write it down immediately.

He leafed through everything again, all the papers he'd tucked inside the Lowrie ledger, hoping he'd missed something the first time, but everything was gone – his Gospels and the few brief notes he'd made before his fall for his survey of the island; the Summons; Flett's speech, which had been written out on the back of the Parable of the Wheat and the Tares. Even the ledger's blue linen binding had fallen apart, and every piece of paper he picked up resembled a hopeless watercolour, or a bruise, all of them the same blotchy mess of black and grey and dirty brownish-yellow.

The big bearded man, Ivar, was watching him turn over the pages.

'Who does he think I am?' thought John Ferguson.

He really was very large, as Strachan had told them he would be, and as John Ferguson turned over the last of the sea-washed pages with his raw and damaged fingers, he began to regret that he had come.

Having been alarmed by the factor's insisting he brought the pistol, he wished now he had it with him. It was a terrible thing to admit to himself, and to God, but it was true. He would have been less afraid with the gun in his possession, and in his weakened state without it, and without Flett's speech, and without the document of Removing to wave about and prove his authority, he shied away from trying to explain his errand.

19

Ivar could never say for sure exactly when he began to transfer his affections from Mary to John Ferguson.

He could never say if it happened little by little in the course of those first few days while his unexpected visitor drifted in and out of sleep, or when he found himself, one evening, reaching for the stranger's battered black coat, wanting to repair it.

He could never say if it happened on the morning of the fourth day while he watched John Ferguson shuffling unhappily through his dried-out papers, but the feeling he had was that it happened quite suddenly, just before that – when John Ferguson woke up and lifted his head and looked at him, for the first time, squarely in the face.

What's undoubtedly true is how powerfully he was affected in that moment – that nothing, perhaps, could have quite prepared him for it. It was so long since anyone but Strachan had looked at him properly, and if he'd been asked to describe his feelings he might have reached for that word in his language that described what happens when a rock is covered and uncovered by the sea – when, briefly, the water rises up and submerges it completely before it falls away again and reveals it. It was how Ivar felt when the wave of emotion crashed over him. He was engulfed by it. His breathing stopped and there was a long, stalled moment before he broke free and breathed again.

When John Ferguson gestured to him to pass him his papers he gave them to him and then he sat in his great chair, watching him.

Afterwards in the outhouse he sorted through the potatoes, conscious of their thick, coarse peel beneath his fingers. He shooed away the mice and the hens. He touched his beard and studied different parts of himself he could see – the splits and grooves on the backs and palms of his hands and the wisps of wool that were caught in them; his legs and his bare feet and the muscle at the root of his thumb. It made him dizzy, the thought of someone else's eyes upon him.

When he came back inside John Ferguson was lying down flat on the bed again but his eyes were still open.

Ivar dried a small quantity of corn in the pot over the fire and ground it roughly and stirred it into a bowl of milk, and while it was warming he stepped over to the bed and eased his hands under John Ferguson's armpits and lifted him a little so he could feed him. But the effort of looking at his papers must have worn him out, because by the time the porridge was ready he was sleeping again, and Ivar pulled the big woollen shawl up to his chin and fetched another peat from the ledge outside and put it on the fire and moved his great chair to the side so it wouldn't be in the way of the heat.

While John Ferguson lay quietly, he sat at his spinning wheel, smoothing out and thinning the yarn, alternately looking at his work and glancing over at the bed, unable to quite shake off his fear that at any moment he might look up and find that his visitor had disappeared.

It was a while since he'd looked at the dark-haired woman in the leather frame, or carried her inside his jumper. He had lost interest in her, and, his only concern now being that the man should not be reunited with her, he put her on the high shelf above the door, behind the teapot, so that only a tiny brown sliver of the frame was visible if you stared hard at the stone wall.

She seemed like a ghost now, like someone from a long time ago, or who was very far away, or dead, more remote than his mother and his grandmother and Jenny, who'd gone to Canada; more remote than Hanus or his other brothers who'd drowned before they were men.

20

After saying goodbye to John in Aberdeen, Mary returned to Perth and the small two-room cottage on the Lowrie estate that was theirs while John was carrying out his duties assisting the factor, Mr Strachan.

Her plan was to stay a week or so, and then continue south to Penicuik by the cheapest means possible and spend the rest of the time with Isobel and Andrew because she didn't want to be a month in Perthshire on her own without John.

It was amazing how quickly she'd come to want to be with him at all times; hard to believe that in all the years she'd been alive she had only known him for four of them. It was almost as if her experience of time had been different, and as she travelled the uncomfortable road from Aberdeen to Perth she thought of a lecture she'd once attended at the Assembly Rooms on George Street in Edinburgh. Attracted by its irresistible title, *The Mysteries of Outer Space*, she'd gone away from it with the knowledge that a single day on Venus lasts almost as long as an entire year on Earth. Watching, now, through the window of the slow-moving mail coach the passage of trees and houses, people, animals and bridges, it occurred to her that her life with John had been like that; as if, in the midst of all the ecclesiastical drama of the past few years, they had still somehow, in spite of the busyness and anxiety of the past few months, managed to live in the eye of it, at some sort of slower centre of it all, on a different planet of their own.

She'd never thought she would marry; had never expected to meet anyone she would love as much as she loved John.

For a while, when she was young, there'd been Angus Souter, turning up every other day at her father's house with only two topics of conversation: his dogs and the price of resin and tar and anything else to do with his family's floorcloth business in Peebles. After every visit Mary would run down the street to find her friend Alice Monk and the two of them would lie on Alice's bed doing imitations of Angus Souter, laughing until they could hardly speak.

For a long time Mary was certain she couldn't be happier than if she'd been able to live the whole of the rest of her life with Alice, the two of them in a small house of their own, but when Alice was nineteen she married and sailed with her new husband to Calcutta, where she died.

After that, Mary generally preferred her own company.

She went for long walks in the Pentland Hills and spent afternoons at the free library in Penicuik. She attended public lectures in Edinburgh and in any other places that weren't too far away to justify the trip. On Sundays, after church, she had supper with Isobel and Andrew and their noisy young family at their square, pretty house next to the Armstrong paper works.

When her father died, the debts revealed in his will came as a surprise and she lived carefully, after the sale of his assets, in a small rented house on the edge of town, always thinking that sooner or later someone like Alice Monk might turn up in some corner of her life, someone interesting and good with a knack of making her laugh, but nothing like that happened; Isobel invited a series of dull bachelors to supper on Sundays, and everywhere she went she came across men who paused to speak to her – men striding over the Kips from Silverburn who wanted to tell her about the best paths; men browsing the most serious-looking bookcases at the library who made rec- ommendations as to what she should read; men who took their seat next to her in draughty assembly halls and talked through the whole lecture so she couldn't concentrate on what was being said, and occasionally she bumped into Angus Souter in the street with his wife and thanked her lucky stars that she had not caved in to the combined pres- sure of Isobel and her father to marry him.

And then the crisis with her teeth had come along, and she'd met John.

She was forty-three, and the Penicuik dentist – trying to soften the blow perhaps – said it wasn't unusual for a woman's teeth to suffer from having children, which made her realise he was confusing her with Isobel.

He could relieve her pain, he told her, by taking out some of her front teeth, two at the top and three at the bottom.

Mary nodded.

She had never thought of herself as vain, but she thought now that perhaps she was.

It was almost unbearable, the picture that came into her mind of herself with only some of her teeth. Vividly, she saw Alice, lying with her mouth open, the two of them holding their stomachs and laughing over Angus Souter and his floorcloths.

When the dentist, Mr Howe, said he could make her some new ones – porcelain in an ivory setting – for twenty-five shillings, she laughed, because what else was there to do? She couldn't possibly afford such a gigantic sum.

The dentist leaned back in his chair then, and put the tips of his fingers together and said he might be able to do them for less, if she was open to an experiment. Mary said she was always open to experiments, and the dentist went on:

'I have a cousin, Miss Law, in the United States, who is an engineer at the Eagle India Rubber Company in Woburn, Massachusetts.'

This cousin, he said, had a friend, a Mr Goodyear, who had invented a substance he called 'vulcanite rubber', which was not yet patented but made a very good alternative to ivory when it came to the setting of false teeth. If his cousin could get him some, he could probably make her a set of dentures for as little as seven and sixpence.

Her new teeth were in her mouth when one of the Comrie earthquakes struck (the big one that caused a breach in the dam near Stirling) – *BOOM!* – as if the small public hall where she was sitting had been smacked by a giant hand or crashed into by some enormous invisible object, bringing down the ceiling in a shower of laths and plaster and sending door handles and window glass flying. Her chair collapsed beneath her and her new teeth shot out of her mouth, and in the dust and debris she couldn't find them.

It seemed like an exceptionally bad piece of luck, to lose so many teeth in a single year, but as she brushed the powdery white mess from the broad skirt of her dress a tall, thin, serious-faced man in a white neckcloth and a black buttoned coat appeared in front of her, carrying her teeth aloft like a crown, or a rescued child, asking if they were hers.

21

While the big quiet man spooned a kind of dusty porridge into his mouth and tucked his blanket in round him, John Ferguson nervously turned over possible explanations he could offer for his presence.

'I could tell him I'm a minister of the new Free Church of Scotland.'

That, as far as it went at least, had the virtue of being true.

As soon as he was able to make himself understood, he could tell the man he'd come for no other purpose than to talk to him about Jesus Christ, and the more he thought about it, the more he wished that *was* true. What better reason to have travelled all this way, and to so lonely a place, than to proclaim the scriptures?

Indeed, he'd begun to feel a growing sense of irresponsibility around his own silence in this department. It bothered him that he had no idea which day of the week it was – that the Sabbath must have come and gone, perhaps more than once, without them observing it. Certainly, he'd never seen Ivar interrupt his work or lay down his tools for any prolonged period, let alone an entire day of rest. It was hard not to fantasise about acquiring enough of his language to at least lead him in a few short prayers. But it

seemed an awful thing to use the evangelical purpose of
the Church as a pretext for his visit; a means of keeping
the peace until Keane arrived. He also had a sneaking suspicion that God was already angry with him for setting
out on so worldly, so material, a mission. Why else would
He have tossed him about on such a terrifying sea and
then hurled him from the clifftops? *Therefore I say unto you,
Take no thought for your life, what ye shall eat, or what ye shall
drink; nor yet for your body, what ye shall put on* – Christ's
words went round and round in his head, reproving him
for being so worried about money, and yet here he was, as
anxious as he'd ever been about how he and Mary would
manage in their straitened circumstances.

Perhaps he could say he was an egg collector?

The doctor at his old parish outside Dundee was always
racing off to the Western Isles to hunt for beautiful and
unusual specimens – surely there was no reason why he
couldn't be doing the same thing here? He could say he'd
been dropped off to spend a short time prospecting, and
that he would be fetched away in due course.

If not that – what else?

A map-maker? A census enumerator? As a minister it
had been his responsibility to return the census, and it
was surely not unimaginable that he might have been
dispatched by the Registrar General to count the island's
human population.

He wished Mary were here. She was always calm and
decisive in a crisis, and in her absence he lay on Ivar's
bed, weighing the various possibilities against each other,
favouring one over another and then changing his mind
again, alternately thinking any one of them would do and

the next moment that none of them would, until, like a lost traveller in a dark wood coming suddenly upon a path, he recalled that Strachan, in his brief description of the island's topography, had mentioned the foundations of an old Viking settlement and the existence of an ancient hermit's cell.

He could say he was an antiquarian.

Yes, he liked that.

If he had to be an impostor, then saying he was an antiquarian seemed to John Ferguson to be the best thing he could be, closer to who he actually was than either an egg collector or a census enumerator. It should not be too difficult, with a few simple gestures and charades, to make the man believe he was here to poke around in the peat bogs and the stony rubble of the island to see what he could discover.

Yes.

As an antiquarian he wouldn't need Flett's speech or the Summons, and it wouldn't matter that he had left the pistol in the Baillie house with his box; as an antiquarian he would be safe, and he could delay the delivery of his message until the *Lily Rose* returned to bring them both away, and in the meantime he would ask God to forgive him for his cowardice and his lies.

22

The spring Jenny's baby was born, Strachan had come and told them there was a new plan for what they would do from now on with the sea-wrack. Nodding with his arms folded, he'd stood on the step in front of the Baillie house while an old Shetlander with a patchy grasp of their language, who'd come with him, explained the details.

The Lowrie factor had shown them how to dig the pits and line them with stones and fill them with wrack and cook it and stir it with the long iron spikes he'd brought, and how to leave it to cool and then break it up into the oily blue lumps he would come back to collect.

He would sell it, he told them via the old man, for the making of glass and soap and for the bleaching of linen, and although they never saw the glass, or any of the bleached linen, they did once see a bar of soap because on one of his visits Strachan gave a piece to Jenny.

Cooking the wrack was filthy, arduous work, and while they did it they had none to spread on the ground for their barley and their potatoes, and both failed, first the barley and then the potatoes, and in the middle of it all the terrible night came when his brothers went out in the boat to the fishing grounds and were lost.

The third winter, with the dried mutton eaten and their

corn used up, and not even any of the meal left that they'd got from Strachan in part exchange for their work – with the birds gone and the weather too wild for fishing off the rocks – they'd survived by drinking blood straight from the sheep, and on limpets and a meagre supply of hen eggs, except for his father and Jenny's little boy Magnus, who they buried a week apart in the cemetery. When the Lowrie minister came the following year he'd said a few words in English over the spot, and Strachan had given them the news that there would be no need any more to gather and cook the wrack because the bottom had fallen out of that particular market and they could go back to using it on their crops and their pasture.

After that Strachan had come back twice, first the following summer and then the one after, asking for rent – for feathers and woollen goods and the cuffs and collars the women embroidered for a shop in Aberdeen, or anything at all they could pay with – but with Ivar's brothers drowned and his father gone, they'd had a miserable time of it. The small flock of sheep did all right, they were tough and independent, but even with Pegi they hadn't enough hands to work the land.

'I'm sorry, Ivar,' said his mother, one arm lifted towards the white hill and dropping down towards the pool where she and his grandmother had begun getting rid of the pups. 'It won't sustain us any more.'

'It will sustain me,' he said.

He was twenty-something then and he was more than forty now, and in all those years Strachan had not come back.

Every summer in the beginning Ivar had expected him, and he'd waited three years before he broke into the Baillie house through one of the windows, thinking he would bring home anything useful. But as soon as he was inside he knew he didn't want to be in there. It reminded him too much of the scar-faced factor and the old minister, and when he surveyed everything the house contained – the table and the bed, the stool and the cooking pot and the good sharp peat shovel round the back – he realised he didn't want any of it.

In the early dawn he stepped outside.

He'd hardly been out since the day he'd brought John Ferguson home, but today while John Ferguson slept he went into the homefield and began to weed the enclosure where the young cabbages were growing, pulling out wall-barley and conium, oat-grass and hemlock and throwing them in a heap against the wall for burning. Then he fetched Pegi from the byre and they brought the peats home from the round hill and he stacked them on the ledge outside the house, and when he'd finished he walked up by himself to the top of the peaked hill and looked out across the water.

Far below, the sea heaved and slapped against the rocks, one long swell after another. Further out it broke over the skerries and eddied between them. Above, he could hardly see the sky for the mass of gannets lifting.

He had not thought of himself as being lonely, or even alone.

He had never regretted what he'd done and had grown used to being by himself. It had not felt like a decision,

or a choice, and in that sense it had not been hard. There
was nothing that Jenny, or his mother, or his grandmother
had been able to say – no picture of another life they'd
been able to paint – that any part of him had been able to
respond to.

Which isn't to say he didn't long for them, or think about
them, or try to see them in his mind's eye or wish they
hadn't left. It isn't to say he didn't sometimes stand inside
the thick stone walls of the house and try to summon the
sensation of being surrounded by people he loved. It isn't
to say he didn't feel a little low when summer began to give
way to the slow beginning of winter; when it was the end
of the short nights and the beginning of the long ones,
when most of the birds were gone and the geese had not
yet arrived, and he said to Pegi, 'Well, Pegi, it is just you
and me again,' – Pegi who'd been given to him when he
was a boy and whose name he'd been allowed to choose;
Pegi who was his helper and his constant companion and
was even older, now, than the black cow.

Last winter, when he'd been ill, he'd thought about his
own death, and what it would be like for there to be no
one to wash him as his mother and his grandmother had
washed the skin-and-bone bodies of his father and Jenny's
little boy, and wrap him as they'd wrapped them in a knitted shawl and lower him into a hole in the island's cool
familiar earth and cover him over with a quilt of soil and
stones.

And yet he'd hated the few occasions, over the years he'd
been by himself, when people had come – the Norwegians
a couple of summers ago who had slept on his floor and
smoked nearly all his tobacco; the boatful of men who'd

spent an afternoon on the cliffs shooting their guns into the air and watching the birds explode from the rocks into the sky; the fishermen from he-didn't-know-where who'd stolen two of his sheep and Pegi's tail, and had come and gone before he could catch them.

Now this.

First the woman in the picture who had stirred his feelings so powerfully but whose reality had somehow faded since the arrival of the man.

He stood for a long time in the softly falling rain and eventually he spoke to himself silently inside his own head:

'I have the cliffs and the skerries and the birds. I have the white hill and the round hill and the peaked hill. I have the clear spring water and the rich good pasture that covers the tilted top of the island like a blanket. I have the old black cow and the sweet grass that grows between the rocks, I have my great chair and my sturdy house. I have my spinning wheel and I have the teapot and I have Pegi, and now, amazingly, I have John Ferguson too.'

23

Ivar shrugged his shoulders when John Ferguson drew the shape of a hermit's beehive cell in the air with his hands.

When he made the same shape directly over his head, wincing as he did so from the pain in his ribs, Ivar looked back at him blankly.

'It would probably help if I put my hands together in prayer,' thought John Ferguson, but it seemed wrong to make a charade out of a sacred act, and he shrank from resorting to it.

Changing tack, he pointed at the bothy walls and put on a pantomime of turning stones over in his hands and looking at them closely, and scratching his head, and making notes with an imaginary pen on top of his knitted blanket.

But whatever lines and curves John Ferguson drew in the air to try and explain his presence, Ivar didn't seem to understand what he meant by them.

What he seemed to believe was that he was being thanked for his hospitality; that his guest was telling him how grateful he was to have a roof over his head, and that this – as far as John Ferguson could tell from Ivar's curt and solemn nod – was enough.

*

Mary's husband had been reunited, by this time, with the rest of his clothes – his trousers and both his shirts, his two sets of underwear and even his white neckcloth and his missing left shoe.

Ivar had found the shoe on the ground not far from the furthest of the two springs; the garments nearby, clinging to the heather and being worried by the wind. He'd brought them home and, like the coat, he'd dried and repaired them, all except the shoe, which was undamaged and which he placed on the hearth next to its partner.

Putting on the clothes had been a challenging operation, however, with John Ferguson insisting on dressing himself until it became clear that he couldn't do anything without Ivar's help. He couldn't stand up, and he couldn't stretch far enough with his arms to pull on either his underwear or his trousers, and his ribs were too sore for him to make the movements needed to put on his shirt by himself. It embarrassed him to be ministered to in this way. No one had helped him dress since he was a little boy, not even Mary. Nothing was as awkward as when Ivar came with the cooking pot and turned him on his side to help him urinate; nothing was as bad as when Ivar's hands were splashed in the process, or when John Ferguson missed the cooking pot entirely and Ivar had to return with his brush and sweep the puddle on the floor into the drain in the corner of the bothy while John Ferguson turned his face to the wall.

He still slept for long periods during the day and night, so much so that he could hardly tell the difference between them. Sometimes when he woke and looked up through the opening in the roof he could see what he thought was the moon, a strip of pearly light between the clouds, but then it would brighten, and as he gazed upwards with half-shut eyes at the dazzling whiteness he wondered if after all it wasn't the sun.

Sometimes when he woke Ivar was there and sometimes he wasn't. When he was there he was always doing something – gutting fish, or chopping hot potatoes on the table, or paying out a loose thread of carded wool in his hand, or sitting in his chair, knitting. It was never fully light inside the bothy, the only opening apart from the hole in the roof being the door, which was sometimes closed and sometimes not. Much of the illumination came from the fire when it was lit, and occasionally Ivar would bring out the foul-smelling lamp. Once, when he opened his eyes, he saw in the gloom the coppery gleam of a fish on the table before Ivar pressed it flat with a crunching sound of bones and began separating the close-packed flesh with his hands. Another time he saw him lift the skin that had gathered on the surface of the milk with his finger and eat it. Sometimes he could hear him digging outside – the sharp scrape of pebbles against his spade.

Ivar was not garrulous. He did not speak often, and when he did his sentences were short.

Woven through them were a few words John Ferguson thought he recognised – a handful that sounded like 'fish', 'peat', 'sheep', 'day', 'look', 'me', 'I', but delivered in an accent that made it impossible to be sure. Anything familiar was hard to pick out because of the way it was woven so tightly with so much he didn't know and couldn't guess, and as a result most of what Ivar said to him in the beginning was incomprehensible, with all meaningful communication consisting mainly of pointing.

After a few days, though, they started to be able to speak to each other in a simple, noun-filled way. Ivar's knitting needles were his *wires*. A *hesp* was a skein of yarn. The box in which he kept his bait was his *kilpek*. The fish-liver puddings he made were *krus*; the porridge was *lik*.

John Ferguson's ankle wasn't broken, it turned out, but it was badly sprained and at the end of the first week it was no less swollen than before. Still, with nothing to do in the bothy but keep his secret safe, he was desperate to get out of bed, and after a few days of trying he could hobble about slowly with the help of an iron spike Ivar gave him as a crutch and called a *hek*.

It hurt to put his weight on the foot of his damaged leg, but with the *hek* he could walk around in the homefield and even up as far as the outfield, and eventually he was strong enough to be able to follow Ivar and Pegi to the foot of the peaked hill, where he waited with the horse while Ivar went to the beach with his bait box for limpets and to fish off the rocks, or to fetch grass for the cow's evening fodder.

Along the way, he began making mental notes for his survey for Strachan – anything that would contribute to his account of the quality of the pasture and its extent, the presence of heath and moor, of large boggy areas unsuitable for grazing etc.

But mostly, as he hobbled along, he thought about Mary, and the new Free Church, about the great distance they had come and the great distance they still had to go. He thought of the wonderful painting the artist David Hill was preparing that would commemorate this new beginning, and he imagined a day, which already seemed less far away than before he came here, when he would have his own church again and he and Mary would have a place to live.

Every once in a while, when they came to a rocky promontory or a large stretch of stony grassless ground, he forced himself to remember them for his report, and in between these occasional observations for Strachan, and his dreams for the future, he engaged in a desultory to-and-fro with Ivar, asking the big bearded islander what words he used for the things they could see around them.

The easiest ones were those for birds and fish and vegetation because Ivar could show them to him as they walked, and if John Ferguson could identify them, everything was straightforward:

Surek. Lorin. Flodrek. Klonger. Hirvek.

Sorrel. Cormorant. Limpet. Wild rose. Loon.

Hogla. Longi. Horseheuv.

Hill pasture. Guillemot. Marsh marigold.

Colours were easy too, because they were there, in front of his eyes on the animals and the plants: *emskit* was a bluish, dusky grey; *dombet* was dark grey; *broget* was pied, variegated.

Other words were harder because there were so many to do with the variations in the weather and the wind and in the behaviour of the water that seemed to mean something very distinct to Ivar but that John Ferguson couldn't confidently define, or that left him flummoxed – words like *gilgal* and *skreul*, *pulter* and *yog*, *fester* and *dreetslengi*, all of which appeared to have a precise and particular meaning that was beyond his experience or powers of observation; all of which, with a slight sense of defeat, he translated collectively as 'a rough sea'.

But those he was reasonably sure of he began to jot down with his pencil – the way they sounded to his ear – on the smudgy sea-rinsed pages that had once carried his Gospels and the schoolteacher's speech and the Lowrie Summons of Removing.

At night, in Ivar's bed with the knitted blanket pulled tight round him, he prayed silently, and thought of Mary, wondering what she was doing and if the letter he'd written to her from Kirkwall had reached her safely, and wishing she was here, and also wishing that he could be alone for a few minutes while he thought about her without the man being so close by, sitting in his big chair and hardly ever, as far as he could tell, closing his eyes.

He hoped she was getting on all right with Isobel and Andrew in Penicuik, and that the journey south from Perth had gone smoothly. There had always been a certain amount of friction between Mary and her brother-in-law, who preferred women, when they were wives, to be mothers, and was a little disturbed by those who weren't. But he was a good man, or at least, if he did little real good in the world, he did no harm. He was a kind husband and an interested father and a reasonably fair employer, and these, in John Ferguson's experience, were unusual qualities to find in a single person. And he had seemed genuinely

pained when his offer of a loan to tide the Fergusons over
this difficult period was politely refused. At least, John
Ferguson hoped his refusal had been polite. He hoped he
hadn't come across as high-handed or sanctimonious or
superior. He'd heard Isobel through a door once, asking
Mary if she didn't wish she'd married someone who wasn't
so serious, by which, he was fairly sure, she meant strict
and humourless and dull and generally Presbyterian.

While John Ferguson slept, Ivar took the pages out of
their blue wrapping and turned them over in his hands,
delicately, afraid he might damage the brittle cloth cover
or crack one of the dry and crispy pages or smudge the
writing.

Before the arrival of John Ferguson he'd never really
thought of the things he saw or heard or touched or felt
as words. In the old days, the minister had read to them
from the Bible in a language they didn't understand, and
then shouted at them in a terrible approximation of their
own tongue. But it was strange to think of a fine sea mist,
say, or the cold north-casterly wind that came in spring
and damaged the corn as solid things on a piece of paper
you could touch. He wondered, looking at the columns
of words, none of which he could read – neither the ones
on the left in John Ferguson's tongue nor the ones on the
right in his own – if there was a word in John Ferguson's
language for the excitement he felt when he ran his finger
down the line between the two columns of words, which
seemed to him to connect their lives in the strongest possible way – words for milk and stream and the flightless
blue-winged beetle that lived in the hill pasture; words

for halibut and byre and the overhand knot he used in the
cow's tether; words for house and butter, for heather and
whey, for sea-wrack and chicken.

It was as if he'd never fully understood his solitude until
now – as if, with the arrival of John Ferguson, he had been
turned into something he'd never been or hadn't been for
a long time: part brother and part sister, part son and part
daughter, part mother and part father, part husband and
part wife.

24

In the days that followed, and as John Ferguson's leg continued to improve, Ivar showed him the inlet where he
gathered the sweet grass for the cow who was too blind to
be allowed off her tether to graze by herself.

He pointed out the island's two springs, the near one
and the far one, and the tongue of land he went to for his
limpets.

He showed him the dried-up fishing boat that was
pulled up on to the rocks on the north side of the island
and weighted down with stones. Full of splits and holes
and missing boards, it had belonged – Ivar did his best
to explain – to a family who had left before Ivar's own:
an old man and his wife whose sons drowned with Ivar's
three brothers in a different boat that never came back
from the fishing grounds. Like his grandmother and his
mother and his brother's wife, Jenny, they'd waited until
some fishermen stopped for water, and when the fishermen left they'd gone with them.

And then one day Ivar took John Ferguson to see the
church where once a year the estate's minister – he put his
hands theatrically together in prayer – had gathered them
when he came with the *umbothsman*. He pointed out the

Baillie house below them where the two estate men used to sleep when they visited.

John Ferguson's heart jumped and his insides turned cold.

The blood rushed to his face and he shifted his weight anxiously between his good leg and his bad one, because he knew that *umbothsman* must be Ivar's word for 'steward' or 'factor', and that if he followed him now to the Baillie house his box would be there, in a place to which only the Lowrie factor had the key.

He'd been telling himself daily that he should go down to the house and drag the box out and hide it somewhere; above all, he wanted to retrieve the pistol in case Ivar came across it first, lying where he'd left it in the box on top of the salted meat and Mary's fruit cake.

The trouble was, he and Ivar were rarely apart for long periods, and even when they were, John Ferguson never knew exactly where Ivar had gone, or when he would be back, or if, wherever he was, he had a view of the Baillie house.

At night he'd lain awake wondering if he might be able to slip out without Ivar noticing, but he wasn't at all confident that Ivar ever really went to sleep – even when his eyes were closed and his breathing was steady and quiet, there was a quality of lightness about his sleep that seemed, to John Ferguson, as breakable as glass.

But Ivar was beginning, now, to turn away from the Baillie house, telling John Ferguson with a sharp, dismissive wave of his hand that he never went there. The place was hateful to him and of no interest, and he hadn't set foot in it for years.

*

Ivar pointed out kittiwakes and razorbills and the different kinds of seaweed that grew along the foreshore – the yellow one called *crawtang* and the greenish-black one called *bongtang*, and later that evening he began – with the same pale-red wool he'd used to darn John Ferguson's underwear and trousers and make new sleeves for his torn-up coat – to knit John Ferguson a pair of socks and a cap for his head.

Because sometimes, in the night, John Ferguson would suddenly start shivering so violently that Ivar could hear his teeth clicking against each other, and when he stepped over to the bed he would see in the low firelight that his visitor had drawn his knees up to his chest and wrapped himself in his own arms to warm himself; huddled up, he'd be turned in his sleep towards the fire. The shivering worried Ivar and before he went back to his chair he would check that the cap hadn't come loose from John Ferguson's head, or that the new red socks hadn't slipped off his cold white feet, which did sometimes happen, in which case Ivar picked the socks up off the floor and put them back on.

Everything had become fairly lively since they'd begun adding verbs and adverbs to the nouns in the makeshift blue dictionary – lots of moving around and lots of arm-waving on Ivar's part and as much as John Ferguson could manage with his bruised and possibly cracked ribs; lots of nodding and head-shaking too, and a succession of pantomimes and charades as John Ferguson mimed what it was he wanted to know, and Ivar acted out what he was trying to describe, and between them they inched towards the right words for, say, knitting and spinning and carding the wool; for eating quietly and for eating noisily; for walking quickly and for walking slowly; for shouting and for whispering; for jumping and for shivering; for coughing and sneezing; for crouching by the fire and for shooing away the hens.

But what most delighted Ivar – what more than anything filled him with hope and happiness – was the way John Ferguson greeted him when he came home after being away by himself at the shore or in the homefield or up on the high pasture. After two weeks, his tall, thin-faced guest was always ready with an account of what he'd been up to while Ivar had been out. Still heavily padded with English, the whole thing was an excited mixture of speech and gestures in which John Ferguson told him how he'd been down to the *o* to wash his socks, or that he'd stayed inside because it was *gruggy* out, or that he'd filled the lamp from the *bunki* and cleaned out the *greut*; that he'd a quick *flinter* around, swept up the *flogs* of *snyag* and brought in the *skerpin*, or that he'd picked some *snori* he'd found growing in the *for*, scalded the *flodreks* and drained them and saved the *flingaso* to make soup, and for a little while now had been sitting in the *tur*, going through everything he'd written down so far on the pages of his glossary.

Perhaps anyone on the receiving end of so much lively enthusiasm would have begun to feel that they were in some way the object of it all, and surely Ivar could not be blamed for starting to think, at around this time, that John Ferguson might be beginning to return his feelings.

*

At the end of the second week the weather turned wild again, and when Ivar went out he mostly went alone, conscious all the time now of being different from his usual self.

Whatever he was doing – whether he was fishing off the rocks or gathering tufts of wool from the hill or carrying stones from the empty houses near the shore to mend his walls so his sheep wouldn't get in and eat his cereals and his vegetables; whether he was gutting fish and hanging them out to dry or leaving them to ferment under a pile of rocks; whether he was digging furrows or ditches or milking his ewes or checking the piece of wood in the cow's tether to stop it twisting and strangling her; whether he was pulling up weeds or bringing back armfuls of mown heather and coarse grass from the bank against the long wall at the top of the homefield and tying it on to his roof because the wind had torn it up again; whether he was going to the beach with his fork to collect seaweed and spreading it on the wedge-shaped piece of land next to the homefield where he planned to put his barley next year – he worked with a restless haste, anxious to get back, afraid that while he was gone John Ferguson would leave, or be snatched away, or turn out never to have existed in the first place.

25

Meanwhile, Ellen Reid – wife of the youngest of the Lowrie ghillies – came with her two small boys to help Mary pack before she headed south to Penicuik.

There wasn't much to pack and they were soon finished – Mary telling Ellen what good boys she had, which was true; both of them stood quietly at the door watching the women work and didn't interrupt them while they talked.

They left the bed linen till last, and while Mary pulled and Ellen tugged, Mary couldn't help saying she wished there was work John could be getting on with for the estate that didn't involve him going on an eight-hundred-mile round trip and being away for a whole month.

She had her two corners of a bed sheet lined up with Ellen's, and as she pinched all four together to fold the whole thing up and lay it on top of the other mending she was taking to Isobel's, Ellen said quietly, as if she was afraid they might be overheard, 'Mr Strachan didnae wantae gang.' He wanted this one off his list, she said. He expected it to go badly, like Tummel Bridge.

Mary stood up straight. 'Tummel Bridge?'

Ellen nodded. It was in the paper. Only an inch or two but it was there. Had she not seen it?

It seemed pointless to Mary, when Ellen had finished

telling her what had happened, to explain that for a while now she and John had been busy with only one story – that every minute of every day had been so full of the great disruption in the Church there'd been no room for anything else in their lives with John rushing about from place to place, and the endless stream of other ministers calling to see him, and all the talking and planning and discussing and the sleepless nights when he was going over everything in his mind and bracing himself for the step he was about to take.

'No, Ellen,' said Mary, 'I didn't see it. Or if I did, I didn't pay any attention. But thank you. Thank you for telling me.'

In Penicuik Mary accosted her brother-in-law as soon as she stepped in through the door.

Why had he not told them about the man at Tummel Bridge? Her face was red and there was a twig in her wild dark hair. She looked as if she had travelled the whole way from Perth in an uncovered cart.

'What man at Tummel Bridge?'

Andrew Armstrong had not been looking forward to his sister-in-law's return; he felt he had gone out of his way to help her rebellious husband and to ease the financial difficulties that were of John's own making. He didn't want either of them staying for what might be an indefinite period in a house that was barely big enough for Isobel and himself and the children, and now here she was standing in front of him on his own carpet looking furious and challenging him about someone he'd never heard of in his life.

'The dead one at one of the Lowrie townships near Tummel Bridge. The factor, Strachan, is reckoned to have got into an argument with him because he wouldn't leave his home when he was invited to. The ghillie's wife told me. It was in the newspaper.'

Not in any newspaper he'd read, said Andrew. 'I know nothing about it, Mary.'

It did ring a bell though – he recalled now that Strachan had been in court over it. Things had gone his way in the end, but no doubt old Lowrie had rapped him smartly on the knuckles for overstepping the mark.

He told Mary he did vaguely remember the incident, but it was a good while back, a year ago at least.

'Well. I think you might have mentioned it,' said Mary.

Upstairs she unpacked her nightgown and sat down on the bed looking out through the window at the smooth folds of the Pentland Hills which had so often been her escape from Penicuik in the years before the Comrie earthquake.

In their private world she and John always referred to this period in their lives as 'B.C.', or at least Mary did, and even though John pretended to be cross when she used the expression – when he became what she called 'all ministerial' and tried to tell her off for being flippant – she knew that they both felt the same way: that there was a Before Comrie and an After Comrie; that their lives were divided into two parts, the part before they met and the part since.

Later, at supper with Isobel and Andrew, she passed dishes when they were asked for and spoke when she was spoken

to, but otherwise not at all, and was generally uncoopera-
tive and badly behaved.

But she was much calmer than before, when she'd
harangued Andrew in his study. Her hands, which had
been shaking then, were still, and she wasn't nearly so red
in the face because she knew, now, what she was going
to do.

26

Sand eel, oystercatcher, tern.

Coalfish, puffin, violet, silverweed.

Ivar pointed to them and reeled off the words in his language and John Ferguson wrote them down in English. 'Coalfish' and 'silverweed' were, admittedly, a bit of a guess – it was a long time since he'd been so close to the sea – but he thought there was a fair chance he'd got them right.

He could name many things now without consulting his blue book: the homefield and the outfield; the place where the peats were stacked, and the place beside the wall where the ground had been raked up; the lamp; the spinning wheel; the white moss Ivar scraped off the rocks on the peaked hill to make his red dye; the hole in the corner of the bothy where the dirty water ran out; the sour perfume of the cow's litter; the dark waste liquid in the byre.

Leaning on the iron spike, he walked along the shore with his trousers rolled up while Ivar fished off the rocks with his many-hooked line. His limp was less pronounced now, and as he moved through the shoal water that was trimmed by the surf he enjoyed the pleasant push and froth of it against his shins.

He'd given up trying to explain his antiquarian's iden-
tity to Ivar, who seemed content for one day to turn into
the next and for him to keep adding more and more words
to his glossary on the dried-out pages of his blue book,
and if this did not seem, to John Ferguson, to be entirely
the right way to proceed, it didn't seem entirely the wrong
one either.

His talk was full of mis-formed nouns and badly made
verbs, and Ivar laughed sometimes at his pronunciation,
which was a little irritating.

But as the days passed he began to mind that less,
and he liked it when Ivar bent forward slightly in his big
wicker chair with his large hands on his knees, listening
attentively and effortfully to his error-laden accounts of
how he'd been busying himself while he'd been at home
and Ivar had been out working.

There were days when the sun was only visible as a luminous spot behind the clouds.

There were days when the mist fell like a cloak on to
the island's shoulders; when rain fell in big, coarse drops,
melting the soil into a soft brown soup; when a cold, light
wind blew low over the ground, making the bogs shiver.
There were days when the weather was so wild that dense
sea-foam was driven over the land across Ivar's fields,
damaging them, and it was too rough for Ivar to do any
work. From inside the house they could hear the thump
of the waves, and when John Ferguson went with Ivar to
look down at the sea from the clifftops they watched the
blue-green water seethe and bubble around the skerries

and the spray being thrown up as the wind took hold of the breaking waves.

But when the weather was fine and the air was almost still and a whitish vapour rose from the ground, or when it was only a little blustery and Ivar could work again, John Ferguson liked following him around, keeping up as well as he could on his bad leg.

In the breeze his papers fluttered and his hair waved about like grass, and every once in a while he reached up with his free hand to try and plaster it back down on top of his head and over the small bald patch at the back where Ivar had cut it away around his wound. Sometimes he stopped and bent over, pressing his hand into a stitch at his side, gulping the air and flapping his arm at Ivar and calling out '*Hipp!*', which was the word he'd heard Ivar use to summon Pegi and the only one he could think of to ask him to please stop, just for a moment, while he caught his breath. Ivar would wait then, until John Ferguson was ready to continue and resume his walking and his pointing at things and his peppering him with questions and making notes on his papers with his pencil.

There was still a lot of repetition and pantomime and charades and back-and-forth between them, lots of trial and error and head-shaking and bouts of incomprehension and frustration, but there were also moments of clarity and understanding, and in the evenings John Ferguson sat down with his rough pencilled lists and made a fair copy of them with his pen and what was left of his ink in the metal writing tin.

Certain words delighted him utterly. The one that

described the condition of a ball of wool, for example, when it had just been started; that described its innermost beginning when a fine thread of worsted was being wound. *Liki.* When the thing was at the very start of what it would become.

At the round hill, Ivar pointed to the first peat he'd cut that had been damaged by the late frost. There was a word, he said, for this outermost, frost-damaged piece of peat that was different from the word for a piece further in and undamaged by the frost, and John Ferguson clapped his hands and said, laughingly, in English, 'Of course there is!'

As they walked, Ivar explained that the barley in the field nearest the homefield had been in its second year of cultivation this year after lying fallow. He pointed to the east side of the island where a dense, almost black mist lay on the surface of the sea. When they got home they ate a pudding made from fish wrapped in the stomach of a slaughtered sheep and in the evening they went out again, for a stroll, and Ivar paused at a spot at the base of the wall below the house through which a stream ran. All these things – the field, the mist, the pudding, the wall with the stream running through it – John Ferguson had words for now, and knew that they were different from the words Ivar had which described other sorts of fields and other kinds of mist; a pudding that was not wrapped in the stomach of a sheep; a wall with no stream running through it.

And here was the difficulty, especially when it came to the weather and the water: for every new word Ivar gave John Ferguson, there always seemed to be another one that described a slightly different version of the same thing but which all too often – to John Ferguson – looked like exactly the same thing.

He still couldn't differentiate, for example, between the great number of words that to him seemed to denote 'a rough sea'. Nor could he separate a *gob* from a *gagl*, a *degi* from a *dyapl*, a *dwog* from a *diun*. He translated them all as 'a miry bog' or 'a muddy swamp'.

Meanwhile a fog could be a *skump* or a *gyolm*, a *blura*, an *ask* or a *dunk*, unless of course it was a mist, in which case it was a *syora* or a *mirkabrod* or a *groma*, a *rag* or a *nombrastom*, a *dalareek*, a *himna*, a *yema*, or a *dom*, and every time he used one of them to describe what he was looking at (even when he was sure it was the dense black kind, which he knew the word for), it seemed to be the wrong one.

Ditto for the clouds and the wind – a cloud could be a *ga* or a *glob*, a *homek* or a *benker*, an *elin* or a *glodrek*. The wind could be a *binder* or a *gas*, an *asel* or a *geul*, and a string of other things he couldn't remember.

Still, it was satisfying to see his glossary of words growing every day – satisfying to gather his pages together at the end of an evening and wrap them up in the rectangle of dark-blue linen that had once covered the Lowrie ledger, and in a small way it helped lighten the gloom he felt over the loss of his Gospels.

In some ways, it felt like a similar sort of project – working hard to turn words from one language into another with all the accuracy and precision you could muster.

He'd been a young minister in a small parish outside Dundee when he'd begun what Mary called his 'Great Project': his own translation of the Gospels into Scots, because he'd wanted to render at least part of the Bible in the language most of the people who came to his church actually spoke. The Gospels, it had seemed to him, would be both a lovely and an essential place to start. Full of poetry, they were what had drawn him, more than anything else, to the Church. Without the Gospels, he thought, it was possible he might have become a lawyer or a schoolmaster or, like his friend Adam Grant, a doctor.

His own command of Scots was decent but far from confident, his vocabulary full of holes, his pronunciation uncertain, his delivery stiff and self-conscious. When others spoke it quickly he regularly lost track of what they were saying; growing up in Dundee with his aunt, and then in Fermanagh with his father, he'd spoken only English.

He'd been forbidden by both to speak Scots, and it was only with his aunt's housekeeper, Annie, when he was a boy, that he'd spoken it at all. Years later, when his aunt was dead and he was back near Dundee as a minister, he'd invited Annie to keep house for him at the manse, consulting her on his word choices as he toiled over his translation.

How delighted she'd been when he told her he planned to have Satan speak in English!

It brought a smile, now, to his own face, and as he tidied his papers away in their blue cloth wrapping it occurred to him that Ivar would see the funny side of that too, and he found himself wishing he had the vocabulary to tell him.

He had never heard Ivar laugh at anything other than his own mangled efforts to speak his language, but he would like to. He had begun to look forward to his smiles, which came rarely, but when they did they were radiant, and he couldn't help feeling, more and more as the days passed, that he was the cause of them, and the thought that this might be true made him excited in a way he would not have thought possible.

27

In Penicuik Mary pawned her wedding ring.

She told Isobel that John should never have gone north.

She was certain Ellen Reid was right, that Strachan expected this particular clearance to go badly and did not want it on his hands – that he had looked at her good, unworldly husband and his desperate need for money and thought, 'Here is the fool I am looking for.' The best thing she could do now was to go after him and bring him home before he had a chance to become involved in what she'd come to think of as 'this stupid errand'.

Stepping out of the pawnbroker's into Charles Street, she thought about her teeth.

She'd asked John once if, in spite of him having rescued them and returned them to her in the earthquake, he disapproved of them.

This was before they were married and were writing to each other every day – he from Edinburgh, from his parish in Broughton, she from her small rented house in Penicuik. She'd told him by this time that she was 'a pretty poor sort of Presbyterian'. Nevertheless, she'd been rattled by something that had happened to her in church: in the middle of the sermon, a woman in front of her had stood up and announced that she'd just had a vision of hell where all the people were dressed in jewellery and wigs and wore false teeth.

Penicuik is a small town, Mary had written. *There is no one in it who doesn't know about my vulcanite dentures, but this is the first time anyone has openly criticised me in church for having them.* What, she was curious to know, were John's thoughts on the matter?

John had written back the same day to say he thought the woman sounded like a nasty piece of work and his advice would be to ignore her completely.

When Mary had written a few weeks later, though, to ask if he'd object to her wearing a ring once they were married, he'd taken two days to reply, and when his letter came it said that on the whole he was against that sort of thing, but if she'd be happier with a ring than without one then so was he. Which was, she realised, his way of saying that there was behaviour he tolerated in her that he would never tolerate in himself, or urge upon his congregation; it was his way of saying that although he believed with every Presbyterian fibre in his Presbyterian body that we must all of us strive to be *in* the world, without being *of* the world, she would always be an exception, and that was because he loved her, and couldn't help himself.

Still, seven and sixpence did seem now like an exorbitantly extravagant sum to have spent on her teeth, and she wondered, walking along Charles Street towards Isobel's house to collect her bag before she began her journey, if a better person than she was would have pawned them too.

*

With the money from her wedding ring she paid for a berth on the steamer *Velocity* to take her from Leith to Aberdeen and then north as far as Kirkwall.

At the Port of Leith she stood looking up at the ship's black hull rising before her like a cliff; its rigging and its masts and its fluttering flags and its huge red funnel like a giant sloping tree. Aboard, people waved farewells from behind elegant white railings. 'Right then,' she said aloud.

In Aberdeen she paced the quayside impatiently while other passengers disembarked and made their way into the city and others boarded with their baggage.

How bleak it was!

She'd hardly noticed when she'd come with John to see him off, but she did now. The quay was granite, the buildings were granite, the pavements were granite, and for the first time since leaving Penicuik her spirits sank. She almost wished she'd waited another day before leaving so that a letter from John would have had time to arrive. He'd have written to her from Kirkwall and made sure the letter was posted before he sailed again, and he'd have ended it the way he ended all his letters, by saying, in his tiny money-saving handwriting: *May all the good angels watch over you, my sweet wife, while I am gone*, and although she did not believe in good angels any more than she believed in bad ones, she knew that he did, and it would have cheered her up.

Still, there was something encouraging about the steamer's name being the *Velocity*, and after an hour walking up and down the quay she returned to it, and not long after that they were on their way again.

*

It astonished her, the way the enormous vessel, trailing its torrent of smoke, ploughed through the water. She had never been on a steamer before, nor so far out to sea that you couldn't see any sort of coast, which was what happened after they left Aberdeen when, for a while, the mainland vanished. Looking ahead and behind and all around her, Mary thought that if the sea here had ever touched land, it must have forgotten what that was like.

Then, at a certain point, she began to notice the appearance of small islands as the first scraps of Orkney came into view – low stretches of white and grey topped with green and edged with a hazy line of mist at the base that was paler than the sea. Closer up she could see the folds of cliffs, stained dark at the height she thought the sea must habitually reach. In places the pasture on top of the cliffs sloped down almost to the water, stopping at a clear line where the rocks and sand began. As she looked, the colour of the pasture changed – different shades of green came and went depending on the movement of the clouds and changing patches of clear sky between them. Now and then a long smudge of rain in the distance screened the sun, sending its illumination down on to a band of water along the horizon before it burst through again and lit up the pasture. It had seemed impossible that grass could be so lush this far north and this far out to sea, as Strachan had said it would be, but she saw now that it was true.

At the harbour in Kirkwall she made enquiries, and after chasing various false leads and dead ends she paid for a box-like bunk on a sound-looking trading smack called the *Laura* that would be leaving for Trondheim in three days' time, and secured a promise from the skipper, Mr Baxter, that he would make a stop at John's island and wait while she went ashore to fetch him.

28

From the beginning John Ferguson had been counting off the days on one of the pages of his makeshift dictionary.

This was partly to keep track of the Sundays, and partly to keep a tally of the total number of days he'd been on the island.

Of course he had no idea which days were *actually* Sundays, but as an expression of thanks and faith he'd decided to count his return to consciousness as the first one, which meant he had now been here for three Sundays, days when he put aside his work on the glossary and devoted himself quietly to prayer and contemplation while Ivar continued to go about his chores.

As for the total number of days he'd been here, he assumed that after his fall he'd been unconscious for two, or perhaps even three of them, which meant he'd been here now for either eighteen or nineteen days; that today was either a Wednesday or a Thursday; that Keane, depending on the weather, would be here in around a week's time.

It was either on the eighteenth, or the nineteenth day, then – either a Wednesday or a Thursday, a calm one with a little wind – that Ivar, carrying one of his rough home-made ropes, beckoned to him to follow.

Together they walked to the bottom of the peaked hill

and from there they carried on past the pond, and as they neared the cliffs Ivar, with his eyes on the ground, began picking up feathers and holding them while he talked.

John Ferguson heard the word *umbothsman* repeated several times and nodded guiltily, because ever since Ivar had pointed out the Baillie house he'd known that this was his word for 'factor', and he understood that he was telling him now, that in the days when Strachan had come to collect the rent for the estate, he'd collected a good part of it in feathers.

'So this is it,' thought John Ferguson. 'He is going to tell me he knows I am here on behalf of the estate; that he has worked out that I can have come here for no other reason. He is going to ask me how much rent it is that I am after, and I will have to tell him that I have not come for the rent but to remove him forever from his home, and that by my silence I have betrayed him and tricked him into thinking I am his friend.'

He began to walk more slowly, looking anxiously at the rope and at the same time not wanting to proceed any closer to the edge of the cliffs.

But at the clifftop Ivar stopped, and John Ferguson watched as he tied one end of the rough woven rope round his hips and the other to a metal spike driven into the rock and lowered himself over the side of the cliff.

John Ferguson's own insides dropped in a freezing rush as if he, too, had suddenly gone over the edge.

'Ivar?' he called out, and when there was no reply he shuffled towards the precipice and peered down queasily, his bowels churning, holding his breath.

Below he could see Ivar moving rapidly across the sheer

sea-facing wall from one toehold to another, gathering eggs from narrow ledges in his net, his big, heavy body in the grip of the squeaking rope, which to John Ferguson looked to be made of nothing but plaited roots and heather and to be no more reliable than a knobbly twist of yarn, and certainly not reliable enough that anyone would trust his life to it.

His heart galloped.

'Ivar, be careful!' he wanted to call out.

But he was afraid his sudden shout would disturb Ivar's concentration and he would fall, so instead he closed his eyes, and counted quietly to a hundred, and longed for the whole thing to be over.

He opened one eye.

'Ivar?'

He hardly dared open the other eye, but when he did Ivar was in front of him with his net full of eggs, free of the rope and with one of his rare and radiant smiles on his heavy, lined face.

'Oh my word Ivar,' said John Ferguson, waiting for the galloping of his heart to stop.

'What a fright you gave me there!'

29

The *Laura*'s progress seemed very slow after the *Velocity*.

It was also much colder, or perhaps it was just that everything, this far north, was colder.

When she stood on deck the wind got between the roof of her mouth and the vulcanite setting of her porcelain teeth and into the metal pins, freezing them and making her wince. Even when she was below and put on all her clothes under her coat, she was cold. And she missed John. She missed listening to him creeping around their bedroom in the early-morning dark, trying not to wake her when he got up to work on his Great Project. She missed her own laughter when he stumbled over a chair leg or the bedpost. She missed him trying out different versions of how he thought the Gospels should sound in Scots – his renditions of the stories of Lazarus and Lot, the miracle of the loaves and fishes, the denial of Jesus by Peter, his betrayal by Judas. She missed his cold feet on hers when they climbed into bed, she missed their sometimes successful and sometimes unsuccessful lovemaking.

She'd never paid much attention to her own body until she married John, and she'd been astonished to discover that such pleasure had been hiding there for so long – astonished that it had been there all this time, yet it had taken her forty-three years to discover it. There was a shyness, to be sure, about John that never quite left him, that could make him halting and clumsy, and sometimes unable, but he always behaved as though she was beautiful, and never less than beloved, and even their failures had never seemed to Mary to be in any way terrible. She wished he was here now, their two bodies squashed close and inseparable in her uncomfortable little bunk.

What on earth, she wondered, was he doing now?

She tried to picture him making his solitary way along some rocky path and knocking on the door of a small, low-roofed house with the estate's blue ledger under his arm. She hated to think of him navigating an unfamiliar world by himself. Even in Edinburgh – a city he was supposed to know – they'd been lost so many times during the week after their wedding when he'd been leading the way, setting off for one place and ending up in another, peering into narrow wynds or looking out off sudden bridges into yawning chasms opening on to streets astonishingly far below. They'd been late for their appointment at Mr Adamson's photographic studio at Calton Hill because John had lost his bearings in the New Town. He'd even managed to lead them astray in the Botanic Gardens – three times they'd circled back to the Tropical Palm House trying to find the way out, and although it had been funny at the time, with John saying, 'Oh dear, Mary, I think we will have to spend the night here,' she thought of it now and it didn't seem funny at all; it made her so anxious and afraid she wanted to cry.

30

The calm weather continued, and this, Ivar explained to John Ferguson, was called a *leura*: a lull; a period of short, unreliable quiet between storms.

Ivar took the opportunity to finish mending the broken wall at the far end of the homefield where the sheep kept getting in. He went round the walls of the house stuffing roots and wool into the cracks between the stones. He weeded the cabbages again because however fierce a war he waged against the oat-grass and the wall-barley, they always came back. John Ferguson meanwhile sat outside in Ivar's great chair, enjoying the sunshine and sometimes going off by himself for a walk. But it is in the nature of a lull to give way eventually to a storm, and anyway, perhaps it was always inevitable that John Ferguson, while he was pottering about inside after one of his walks, would one day come across Mary's picture on the high shelf above the door, hidden behind the teapot.

Ivar was outside plucking the sheep, and when he came back with a bundle of wool in his arms John Ferguson was holding the leather-framed picture in both hands. He seemed unable to speak.

When the words eventually came out he shouted them

in English, either too angry or too upset to try to speak to
Ivar in his own language.

'This is my *wife*, Ivar! My *wife*. My own wife, Mary,
who all this time I have been lost without, and who I now
discover you have been hiding from me.'

His expression was severe and the way he spoke
reminded Ivar of the way the estate's minister had thun-
dered at them in the cold, thick-walled church when he
told them about their sinfulness and everything they were
doing wrong in their lives.

Ivar kept hearing the word 'wife', and he didn't need to
understand any English to know what it meant. He could
hear its meaning in the way John Ferguson said it, and anyway he had never doubted that was who the woman was.

He put the wool on the ground and sat down in his
great chair. There were tears in his throat. He wanted to
tell John Ferguson that it was a long time since he'd looked
at the picture of his wife or thought about her in any way.

His tears shocked him. It was years since anything had
made him cry. It was years, too, since anyone had shouted
at him. He turned his face away, into the hearth, reminding himself that irritation and arguments are common
between people who live together; he had only forgotten because he'd been alone for so long. He'd often been
shouted at when he was young, and every once in a while
there'd been stormy outbursts between almost everyone
in his family – between his parents, between his mother
and his grandmother, even, sometimes, between Jenny and
Hanus.

'This will blow over,' he tried to tell himself, keeping his
eyes on the hearth. 'John Ferguson will calm down and

forgive me for hiding his wife from him, and when he's ready he'll take out the blue cloth book and lay it across his lap and ask me to pass him his pencil, and we'll set about the task of adding another column of words on a fresh page and everything will be the same as before.'

It would, surely.

He didn't know what he'd do if it wasn't. What he'd had had always felt like enough, but he was not sure it could feel like enough again if he didn't have John Ferguson here with him any more – he wasn't sure he could be without the back-and-forth of their stumbling communication and not have him close by, not have him inside his own four walls to care for, to prepare food for, to sit with through the evenings and sleep near to during the nights.

Once, before Strachan stopped coming to collect the rent, there was a shipwreck on the west side of the island.

When Strachan and the old interpreter from Shetland arrived with the *Lily Rose* they made it known that if anyone was hiding anything from the wreck, they should bring it out or be prosecuted as a thief.

It wasn't difficult to understand what the old man was telling them: that it was within the Lowrie factor's power to choose whether he punished the miscreants here on the island, or whether he took them with him to the mainland to be tried in a court of law, where anyone who had concealed even the smallest item that did not belong to them would be found guilty and made an example of.

One by one the precious pieces of salvage were brought out – the good, strong rope and the delicious liquor; the useful sailcloth and the hefty lengths of broken timber;

the knives and forks and pairs of scissors and the marvel-lous green dress with the lace collar that Jenny had found floating in the inlet below the church.

But Ivar had already buried the teapot in the place in the round hill where he and his brothers dug the peats, because his grandmother said if he didn't the factor would claim it for the estate, or the Crown, or more likely for himself. She herself had kept hidden a tiny golden bird – no bigger than her own thumb – that she'd found when she was a girl, buried in the ground in an ancient-looking pot with a bundle of bones when they'd gone looking for stones to build the byre. The estate, she said, would have claimed it long ago if she hadn't hidden it, and the same went now for the teapot Ivar had found resting on a mound of wrack with the lid still on, the delicate spout and handle unbroken: a beautiful object his grandmother said was for pouring the tea after you'd boiled it in a pan. He'd run his fingers over the raised white figures clothed in graceful robes, holding spears and standing among trees and surrounded by garlands of leaves and flowers, and then he'd lifted it carefully from the slippery kelp, terrified he would be the one to smash it when it had so miraculously survived the breaking-up of the ship.

From then on, every year when Strachan came for the rent, he'd buried it in the hill and dug it up again when the scar-faced steward was gone. It was only when two, three and then four years passed without Strachan paying his annual visit that Ivar had thought it safe to put the teapot on the high shelf above the door where it shone in the beauty of the firelight and kept him company.

*

He couldn't look at the teapot now without feeling John Ferguson's anger.

For an hour they sat in silence; Ivar in his great chair, John Ferguson on the bed with the picture of his wife next to him on his blanket. Once in a while he picked up his papers and looked at the lists of words on them, but mostly he just sat. Ivar tried to get on with some knitting but kept pausing, trying to think of something to say but at the same time afraid to break the silence between them in case he only hardened it.

He was about to warm some milk, thinking he would offer a bowl to John Ferguson, in the hope that this might return them to where they'd been before their argument, but just as he lifted the pot on to the hook above the hearth John Ferguson rose from the bed, put the picture in his coat pocket, and walked stiffly out through the door.

31

On Shetland they were delayed a whole week in Lerwick while the *Laura* waited for the arrival of various goods going to Trondheim and for another paying passenger, who, like the goods, was also bound for Norway, and who finally appeared after another day and a half.

Most of Mary's money was gone now, used up on eight nights at a cheerless overpriced hotel in a dark street behind the harbour. But at last they were on their way again, and Mary was up early, fully dressed and with her teeth in, her hair brushed and arranged in two heavy loops either side of her face.

It was even colder now than it had been after they left Kirkwall, both inside her tiny curtained berth as well as outside it, and she wore all the clothes she'd brought – both chemises, both petticoats, both pairs of stockings, her hat and her gloves, her short cape and her long coat and her shawl. She felt like an upended bolster, firmly packed and very heavy and difficult to move, but at least she was no longer freezing.

When she was not lying down in the box-like bed of her tiny berth at the stern end of the hatchway, trying to read, or picking her way through the obstacle course of ropes and boxes, sacks, sails and vegetables that crowded the hatchway, she was up on deck, watching the sky and the water and the birds that came and went above them. Sometimes Mr Lane, the other paying passenger, came to stand next to her, which was annoying, because naturally he was curious about where she was heading and why, and the last thing she was going to do was tell him she was on her way to rescue her husband, who had got himself into a difficult situation somewhere in the middle of the North Sea.

Instead she gave him a story about John being on an evangelical mission for the new Free Church of Scotland on one of the remoter islands; the *Laura* was dropping her off there so she could help him.

Mr Lane, who was accompanying a shipment of his own linen to Trondheim, threw his head back and laughed. 'Good luck to you both!' he shouted with an enormous smile into the wind, and predicted that the new Free Church wouldn't last five minutes. It was like a snail without a shell, he said. Its ministers would starve and their congregations would wither away in the absence of anywhere to worship.

Since leaving Lerwick, the linen merchant had spoken to her at length on various topics, some political, some geographical, some botanical, and it was all Mary could do not to put her hand on his arm and say, 'Thank you, Mr Lane, but there was not a single thing in what you just told me that I didn't already know.'

Invariably, he turned eventually to his favourite subject – the weather.

He loved to talk about the storms he'd experienced

over the years in the pursuit of trade across the North and
Baltic Seas, and as the breeze stiffened he began to tell
her about the famous one she already knew about that
had swallowed half the Caithness herring fleet whole, and
sunk three well-built vessels en route between Stavanger,
Riga, Amsterdam and Hull, with the result that no one
had ever seen their cargoes of timber, linseed oil and cod,
nor any of their crew, ever again.

Mary pointed at the thunderous sky and asked Mr
Baxter, the skipper, if the change in the weather was anything to be worried about.

'No,' said Baxter, rolling his eyes so she would know
what he thought of the linen merchant. He didn't think
either the stiffening breeze or the darkening sky were anything to be worried about, and that it would not be long
now before they reached her destination.

'You will see it,' he said. Even when they were still some
way off, she would see the island rising out of the waves
from its hidden beaches. She would see the dark cliffs
and the tricky waters beneath that were dotted with skerries, and if the sun was shining she would also see a gleam
of green.

32

John Ferguson wasn't immediately aware that he was lost.

His exit from the bothy had been a swift, ungainly hobble that took him out past the byre and beyond the homefield and down towards the church, and from there he'd carried on, stumping along over the heather and doing his best not to step into one of the island's hidden streams or fall headlong into one of its quaking black bogs. With his eyes on the ground, he'd paid no attention to where he was going. He was still trembling a little, still trying to recover himself after what had happened back at the house with Ivar and Mary. He slowed down, thinking that would help calm the trembling and slow his heart, and for a while he plodded on, still looking at his own feet, until at last he looked up and found himself in a part of the island he didn't recognise.

When he turned round, he could see the tallest of the three hills – the white one – but while he'd been walking the clouds had come rolling like smoke over the heath and he couldn't see the other two, neither the round one nor the peaked one.

What he could see, above a rocky cove and next to the first tree he'd come across since he'd been on the island, was what he thought must be the hermit's cell – a mound of stones like a tiny prison that really did resemble a beehive.

He crawled inside.

Hunched in the darkness, he sat gripping Adamson's calotype of Mary, and although in the blackness he couldn't see her face, he could picture her smile with its Mary-ish blend of scepticism and self-consciousness.

'I've missed you, my darling,' he said quietly, aware, even as he spoke, that he had not thought about her much in the last few days. It was true though, he did miss her, and having discovered her again he longed to see her; it was only that his strange existence here on Ivar's island had pushed her out of his thoughts.

He began telling her about all the things he'd been turning over in his mind while he lay on his bed at night and when he'd been criss-crossing the island with Ivar: that with the sixteen pounds the Lowrie estate paid him for his work here he would look for some furnished rooms to rent in Broughton where they could live, and once they were settled he'd start hunting for suitable premises for a church. It wouldn't need to *look* like a church; any sound, serviceable building would do, and after the months he'd spent preaching in borrowed parlours and in the street, and that time – did she remember?! – in the rain on the pier at Newhaven, it would feel like a proper beginning.

He paused and tried to pray, but he couldn't.

Outside he could hear the wind, and the sea crashing at intervals against the rocks below.

'I shouldn't have shouted at Ivar this morning,' he told himself eventually. 'It was not an unnatural thing for him

to have done, to want to keep Mary's picture for himself.
I should have been kinder.'

Slowly and evenly he breathed in the damp, peaty
atmosphere.

Across the small round entrance he could see the low,
wind-bent branches of the tree. It was a rowan, he thought.
Its prickly twigs had scraped his face when he'd crawled
inside and his cheeks were stinging.

In spite of the light filtered through the tree's screen, it
was still very dark.

It was also extremely cramped – if he reached out with
his hands, his fingertips touched the walls before he had
fully extended his arms. He patted the cold stone and tried
to imagine what it would be like to spend your whole life
immured in such a minute and gloomy place.

'I could tell Ivar now, why I'm here.'

It was true, he could. They were able to communicate
quite efficiently now, in a broken way – Ivar speaking his
own language while he, John Ferguson, wrestled with his
own tortured mish-mash version of it, still filling in the
gaps with plenty of English and occasionally throwing in
a little Scots, always hoping there was enough that was
familiar to Ivar that he would know more or less what he
was talking about. His vocabulary was growing every day
– he knew the words for the plaited straw mats Ivar placed
between Pegi's back and the loaded baskets she carried;
for the pink thrift that covered the slope above the brook
below the bothy, and for the lady's mantle that grew along
the wall in the homefield that made him think now of the
lady's mantle Mary had planted beside the front path of
the Broughton manse before they'd left it because she'd

liked the way the leaves held the rain, making them spar-
kle as they sparkled here on the island.

But, most importantly, he knew the word for 'ship'; the
words for 'pasture' and 'sheep' and 'mainland'.

He knew the verb that meant 'to leave', or 'go away'.

It would not be an elegant speech, and it would be full
of grammatical mistakes, but it would be clear enough.

And yet he shrank from delivering it. If it had seemed
difficult at the beginning, it seemed impossible now. He
was less afraid of Ivar than he'd been at the start – less
worried that, with his quiet bulk, he would turn violent.
What he dreaded now was how it would feel to have Ivar's
eyes upon him when Keane arrived and began the business of dispatching the livestock – Pegi and the old black
cow and the tough, sure-footed sheep. What he dreaded
was how Ivar would look at him when he finally delivered
his much-postponed message, how he would stand before
him with his mouth a little open, how there would be dis-
belief and bewilderment etched into the heavy lines of his
face, and how by the time they were loading the *Lily Rose*
with his spinning wheel and his tools and his cooking pot
and anything else he was permitted to bring, he would
have turned away from him completely, doing everything
in his power to make sure he never looked at him again.

'I could remind him,' he thought, 'about providence. I
could console him by explaining to him that his suffering,
like all our suffering, is nothing more than punishment
for our sins, that it is God's will, and our Christian duty
to submit to it.'

But crouching in the darkness of the hermit's cell,
John Ferguson couldn't imagine talking to Ivar about

providence. It seemed a shabby thing to him suddenly –
an abdication of his own responsibility, a denial of his own
involvement. All his life he had believed in providence;
he was full of doubt now.

He leaned against the cell's curved wall and pressed his
cheek into the rough and chilly stone. 'I should never have
accepted so many bowls of milky soup from him. So many
warm fires and hot liver puddings. I should never have
allowed him to give up his bed for me. I should never
have accepted the knitted socks and cap and the repairs
to my coat. I should not have spent so many scores of
hours encouraging him to teach me his obscure and difficult language.'

He found himself wishing he could go back and start
again and do everything differently. But time was the worst
thing; time, it seemed to him now, was the only thing you
couldn't change; whatever you did, it kept coming. He ran
his fingers over the leather frame round Mary's picture.

Well.

The end, he supposed, would be here soon enough; it
would not be long now before Keane came.

Blinking, he emerged into the light, pushing his narrow
head through the hole and the tangled branches of the
rowan tree, and when his whole body was out he stood up
and brushed off the crumbly earth and feathers and pellets
of dried excrement his coat had picked up from the floor
of the anchorite's chilly dungeon. Across the island the
smoky clouds had lifted, and with his back to the water he
could see the tops of the two smaller hills to the left of the
white one. All he needed to do to get back to Ivar's bothy
was to head for a point between them.

33

Ivar had waited most of the afternoon before setting off, in the clearing cloud and the rising wind, to look for John Ferguson.

He went first to all the places they'd been together – the beach and the inlet, the rocky spit where he went for his bait, the fowling cliff and the small round bay where the old boat was, and the bottom of the peaked hill where John Ferguson sometimes used to sit with Pegi when his leg was hurting.

After that he went to the church because it seemed like a place someone might go, to be by himself.

But there was nothing there either, only his hay and the cold breeze whipping through the worn-out roof.

He went back outside, and from the burial ground he scanned the pasture all around and then he carried on up the slope until he came to the Baillie house.

Exactly when the wind had succeeded in tugging open the unlocked door is hard to say. For weeks, ever since John Ferguson had headed off so optimistically to bathe and closed it behind him without locking it, it had been shaking and rattling in its loose, half-rotted frame; now it was flapping like a broken wing against the wall.

*

In the hearth were the remains of a failed fire, the peat still more or less intact, a little charred kindling – heather roots and some sticks of hay – and in front of it all, on the stone floor between the stool and the three-legged table, there was a box stamped in white letters with the one English word Ivar knew how to read: LOWRIE

Inside it he found flour and cheese, a few apples and some salted meat and a flint fire striker; a big bag of sugar, and another of tea, and a small one of what he thought was coffee; a half-eaten cake wrapped up in waxed paper, and in among all these sundry groceries and supplies he found a pistol and some ammunition and a horn of damp powder.

He turned the pistol over in his hands, the cold metal and the warm wood.

He couldn't say if it was the same one that used to hang from Strachan's belt, but like that one it was heavy and large, and like that one it had a hook so it could be worn hanging from a man's waist in the same way.

So, he thought, I am like a puffin.

Like a puffin I wasn't frightened of him. Like a puffin I have spent my days swimming beside him.

Like a puffin I have walked about, close to the snare. I have pecked at it and picked it up in my beak and looked at it from different sides and now I have put my foot in it and the string has tightened round my stupid ankle and I am caught.

I have done everything in the wrong order.

I have stayed close and confined within my own four walls and kept to the fishing rocks and the homefield and the high pasture and I have allowed myself to become

attached to him when all along I should have come down
to the Baillie house to have a look around.

How could you, Ivar?

It was his grandmother's voice – stern and critical and
astonished.

He'd heard it many times in his head during the years
that he'd been alone – upbraiding him for the commis-
sion of small errors of judgement or calculation as he went
about his work, reminding him, always, to proceed with
caution in everything he did because there was only him
now in the world, and if he ever tripped or fell or injured
himself or made any kind of mistake there would be no
one here to help him.

If his grandmother could have picked him up and
carried him with her when she left, she would have. If
he'd been a baby or a small boy she would have tucked
him against her shoulder or propped him on her hip and
shown him the tiny golden bird she would sell to buy their
passage to the New World; she would have held him in
place with one of her strong sinewy arms and stepped up
into the boat and sat him down next to Jenny and his
mother. Over the years, he'd often thought about that –
that if there'd been any way she could have bodily lifted
him, she would have.

How could you have been so stupid, Ivar?

He shook his head, as if, suddenly, she was standing
next to him, looking down at John Ferguson's box with
the white Lowrie letters printed on the side. 'I don't know,'
he said aloud, thinking only that one thing had happened
and then another, and that along the way he'd closed himself off from anything that resembled his grandmother's

brisk and bossy voice and the warning reminders that had always, in the past, stopped him doing stupid things.

In his head, Strachan was the *umbothsman*, and to Ivar the pistol had always seemed like a suggestion of what could happen if they didn't produce the required seven stones' weight of feathers, or complained about the estate leaving them with no wrack to nourish their crops. He used to sit, the Lowrie factor, on the step outside the Baillie house and clean the gun with a rag and push the little metal balls and wads of cotton into it and do everything necessary to prime it, and sometimes he'd shot at birds for sport or for his own eating, and once he'd used it to strike Jenny on the side of her head because she didn't want his hands on her and had made her feelings known by biting his face.

He put the pistol back in the box and hefted the whole thing on to his shoulder, and when he got home he went into the byre and put it at the back in the dark.

Then he stepped into the house, where John Ferguson greeted him with a smile to show that he'd forgiven him for hiding his wife behind the teapot, and that everything was all right again between them. With one of his little speeches full of words that were partly right and partly wrong, he said he'd cooked the halibut Ivar had brought home last night and it was ready for them, now, to eat.

34

At this time of year, when it is light for so much of the night, the island feels like an unsleeping place, as if it is only ever dozing through the small hours and nothing could happen anywhere on it, or around it, without it noticing.

Ivar sat in his chair watching John Ferguson sleep, the gentle rise and fall of his breathing.

After they'd eaten, he'd walked down to the shore by himself, leaving John Ferguson with his papers. The swell in the sea was the swell that preceded boisterous weather and came with the gathering of the wind, and Ivar stood and watched the slow heave of the water and tried to let himself be calmed by the freshness of the breeze.

If it had been another year – last year, say, or the one before – he would have had a little to offer in the way of rent: a meagre token at least, something to show willing, a small deposit on a promise to work harder and be more productive in future.

But this year, with his illness, he'd hardly scraped through at all. He'd let almost all the barley go and nearly all the corn. He'd lacked the strength to dig the potatoes beyond those he needed to stay alive. He had no feathers,

not a single solitary sack; until the other day, when he'd
gone to the fowling cliff with John Ferguson, he hadn't
been there once, knowing it was far, far beyond him to
lower himself on the rope from the metal kelp spike, let
alone haul himself back up, which was the method he'd
devised for harvesting the birds and their eggs since he'd
been by himself. Nor, until a few weeks ago, had he plucked
the fleeces of his sheep. He'd done almost no spinning and
less knitting. A few caps and pairs of socks he'd made in
the spring, but that was all. He had no garments to offer
John Ferguson, and although the big store of collars and
cuffs was still here from when Jenny and his mother and
his grandmother used to embroider them for Strachan to
take back with him to the shop in Aberdeen, it was years
since he'd been near them with a needle.

In the byre he pressed his thumb against the pistol's
trigger, but nothing happened, which did not surprise him.
He knew from watching Strachan that there was more to
it than that; you needed to combine the ammunition and
the powder, though where, and in exactly what way, he
wasn't completely sure.

Looking back, he wondered if he had always known – if
it had been clear to him from the beginning that his visitor
must have been sent by the estate, only he had not wanted
to believe it. Looking back, he wondered if the knowledge
had been there from the moment he found John Ferguson
on the beach, and it had been this, more than his feelings
for the woman, that had made him wish, then, that he
would never wake up. Looking back, it was impossible to
unpick how one thing had led to another, and what exactly
he had chosen to see and not to see, and how it was that

he'd been able to convince himself that John Ferguson, with his dark hair and his sharp nose and his serious, anxious demeanour, had come from nowhere and was going nowhere – that he was some aimless traveller who had nothing to do with anything or anyone; that he was just *here*.

Looking back, there was only one thing that was completely clear to him, and that was that he had loved the time he had spent with John Ferguson.

Back at the house, he began cutting the heather that was stacked in a heap against the wall for the roof, but he made a poor job of it, and although he knew he should stop and sharpen his knife, he pressed on until at last he accepted that he was trying to carry out a task which, in his present state of mind, was beyond his power.

He laid down the knife and went to check the *snaver* in the rope round the neck of the old blind cow and stood talking to her for a while.

He stroked the broad, flat plane of her massive forehead, telling her what he could see: a big dark cloud with a whitish top through which the sun was shining, and next to it a bank of smaller, detached clouds. The bad weather out to sea was still some way off, he told her, and everywhere else the sky was light-coloured, like growing corn. There were some puddles on the ground that shivered and glittered in the breeze, and the hens, she would not be surprised to hear, were making a jerky, stiff-footed search around the entrance to the byre, hoping for seeds or grain, or anything else tasty that was lying on the ground or hidden in Pegi's waste.

It wouldn't be hard, he thought, to ask John Ferguson what was going to happen now – he was sure that if he prompted him with a combination of words and gestures, John Ferguson would understand he was asking him to tell him who he was. He remembered the strange hand movements his visitor had made in the beginning, and how he'd ignored them, not wanting to know why he was here because that would involve thinking about how long he would stay and when he would leave, and from the moment John Ferguson had looked him squarely in the face and the wave of emotion had crashed over him and almost drowned him, he'd never wanted to think about him not being here any more.

35

When John Ferguson arrived back from the hermit's cell, he did what he could to make clear to Ivar that he was sorry for shouting at him; that as far as he was concerned, the business with Mary's picture was forgotten.

But Ivar seemed different: remote, sad.

He hardly touched his halibut, and John Ferguson was still eating when Ivar pushed back his great chair and got up and went out. It was late when he came back and turned the chair away from the table to face the fire and sat down and closed his eyes, and when John Ferguson woke up in the morning he'd already gone out again.

Mary's husband spent the morning cleaning and tidying the house.

It was all he could think of to do: to make it welcoming for when Ivar came back.

He folded their blankets and cleaned the cooking pot. He swept the loose grass scattered across the floor into the drain. He went down to the brook and picked a handful of thrift and lady's mantle and put them on the table in the brown jug, and when he stepped outside to fetch peat for the fire he saw Ivar in the homefield talking to the black cow; but although he waited for him to come in, he didn't, and when he next looked outside he couldn't see him.

At first John Ferguson didn't worry; he sat in Ivar's great chair, going through his pages, memorising batches of words and organising them into groups as well as alphabetically – words to do with the weather and the water, with the earth and what was under it; words of a domestic nature. He made a new page devoted exclusively to sounds – to the *hoss* and *horl* of the sea, the *yal* of the gulls, the *tusk* of the wind, the *snirk* of a door.

He went over another batch of words Ivar had given him that had double meanings – words that seemed to interest and excite Ivar more than anything, as if he'd never thought about their richness and versatility until he'd started teaching his language to John Ferguson.

He'd explained, for instance, that his eldest brother, Hanus, had been a big, stout person, and that this single-syllabled word, which had both bigness and stoutness contained within it, also had the meaning of 'a large wave'.

It had taken a long time before John Ferguson had grasped what Ivar was saying, and he had the impression at the end of it all that Ivar was conscious in a way he'd never been before of how right it was: that a word which described his brother physically also described a big wave; as if Hanus had possessed something of the sea's strength. If any of his brothers could have made it back alive, he seemed to be thinking, it would surely have been Hanus.

Another word with a double meaning was the one for when you felt a fish nudging the end of the line, which could also mean, if John Ferguson had understood Ivar correctly, 'a slight impression, or feeling, of something'.

There was also the word for a certain kind of thick mist, which could signify what John Ferguson translated, after a lot of to-ing and fro-ing, as 'a deep pondering'.

Stroda, meanwhile, seemed to describe the backwash of the waves against the steep rocks, as well as great agitation or hurry in a person; a *hobbastyu* was both a turbulent sea and a great difficulty, or dilemma; a *guster* was a strong, drying wind and also, he was fairly sure, a loud, blustery, arrogant way of speaking.

He went through all these new words a second time, and then he went through them again, and after that he slept, and when he woke the afternoon light had changed into that different light by which you know that although it is not yet dark, it is late.

Outside he could hear the old blind cow bellowing in expectation of her evening fodder.

He waited another hour or so, and when Ivar was still not back he went looking for him.

He looked for him first in the outfield, where he might have expected to find him at this time of day, and when he wasn't there he carried on, following the furthest of Ivar's low walls until it ended and he came to the stream and the fertile meadow beyond it. The ground was dry, and he walked quickly between patches of thrift and lady's mantle until, halfway across, the dry ground gave way to a huge flooded area, and soon his feet were soaking wet. He considered going back to the wall and heading in a different direction, but he'd gone too far now into the swamp to turn back and he was already so soaked it seemed better to carry on. The bone in his shin was beginning to ache, and although he tried to take short, light steps to lessen the pain, the boggy ground sucked on his feet and made it impossible. Just before he reached the higher, dry ground after the meadow he stepped in an especially deep puddle of dark slime and cried out, furiously. Meanwhile the wind came in puffs, softly to begin with but then more vigorously, first from one direction, then from another, as if it was deliberately trying to hamper his progress. Up on the high pasture the fleeces of the sheep shook. His own clothes fluttered and billowed as he pressed on towards the cliffs. At the top of the first ghyll he paused for breath while below the sea broke over sunken rocks and foamed around them in greenish eddies. With his aching leg he stood in the cold looking out across the empty water. In his head, going round and round, the word Ivar had given him for something that has disappeared or been lost; something never to be found in spite of searching.

'Ivar!' he called out.

He walked down to the beach on a long, slow path he hadn't come across before which looked easy from above but was in fact rocky and undulating and exhausting and by the time he reached the end of it he was stumbling. He sat on a rock to rest his leg, popping hollow blisters of seaweed between his forefinger and his thumb. There were big heaps of it everywhere, glistening and dark and dirty-looking. At his feet an eel wound itself down into the sand and lay beneath the surface, coiled and buried. It was all very ugly. He got up and continued along the beach and up again on to the pasture until he came to the loaf-like mound of the round hill and the place where Ivar dug the peats, but Ivar wasn't there. Long waves rolled towards the shore, passing over the rocks without breaking and a soft, cold rain began to fall. His leg was really hurting now but he carried on, up to the top of the round hill and down again, and then on to the summit of the peaked one. Everywhere he looked there seemed to be black puddles of thick standing water with stalks of grass poking out of them. He passed the short row of low, connected dwellings that Ivar said had been inhabited when he was a boy. A little further on he passed another one. He went down to the inlet. The surface of the sea had a scraped, scrubbed look. Long, skittish shadows, hurrying in front of the wind, raced across it. Cormorants glinted, gulls hung in the air with their mouths open. Dark, heavy clouds rested on the horizon and he found himself wondering what Ivar would call them – would he say they were *homeks* or *benkers*? *elins* or *glodreks*? He wanted urgently, suddenly, to know the answer, to be able to describe things as they were instead of only guessing at them. Was the thick, drifting mist around the bottom of the white hill a *himna* or a *yema*? Was it a *rag* or a *dom*? Not knowing the right words made him feel as far away and separate from Ivar as he had ever felt since the day he'd arrived. Even in the moment when he'd opened his eyes for the first time after his fall, he hadn't felt as distant from him as he did now. Back then, he had looked at him sitting in his great chair, and even though he was a stranger, he'd had the feeling that in some buried unconscious part of himself, he knew exactly who he was. Now he felt that whatever had connected them before had been broken, or taken away. He went to the fowling cliff where Ivar had terrified him by lowering himself from the metal spike on one of his squeaky home-made ropes and dangled against the wrinkled cliff, a butterfly pinned against a black wall.

'Ivar!' he shouted, shaking in the cold, amazed at his anguish.

'Ivar don't do this! Don't go somewhere and not tell me where you have gone!'

But when he arrived back at the bothy Ivar was there, spooning a lumpy yellowish substance into the clay jug. It looked like a kind of failed butter, grainy and mushy and partially separated.

Ivar didn't look up when he came in, and John Ferguson was so cold and exhausted and frightened by his search he couldn't speak.

'You have been a long time away,' said Ivar quietly.

It was a single word in his language, and John Ferguson didn't understand it. What he did understand was that it sounded neither sulky nor reproachful, and that it was Ivar's way of saying that if there'd been a distance between them, he wanted there to be an end to it.

John Ferguson watched him tip the lumpy butter-like stuff into the iron pot, mix in the meal-dust that had settled on the edge of the small millstone he used to grind the corn and then cook it over the fire, and as soon as it was bubbling they both ate it hungrily.

Where the music came from, Ivar couldn't have said – his memory of any sort of music was as distant as anything he'd experienced when he was young, but the fragment of a tune came back to him as he sat that night with John Ferguson in the firelight.

He started humming it, and as he hummed the memory became sharper and more intense, and more and more of the music flooded his mind until he was singing and on his feet and holding out his hands to John Ferguson and asking him to dance.

John Ferguson's first reaction was to laugh.

'No, Ivar. No!'

He tried to muster the words and gestures to explain that in his Church no one danced. In this respect the new Church did not differ from the old one. Dancing was ungodly and undignified and forbidden, and he was against it. He laughed awkwardly again, wanting, after everything that had gone on earlier, to lighten the moment, but at the same time wanting to make it clear to Ivar that he was declining his invitation. He shook his head and folded his arms and crossed his legs.

Ivar stood with his hands stretched out. He knew from the minister who used to come with Strachan that you weren't supposed to dance; that dancing was wrong and you shouldn't do it. On every one of his annual visits the old Lowrie minister had reminded them that they had been put on this earth to suffer, not to enjoy themselves.

But Ivar was strong, much stronger than John Ferguson, and he kept singing and tugging on John Ferguson's hands until he'd pulled him to his feet.

Slowly, at first, and then more quickly, the walls around them began to spin.

It wasn't like any dancing John Ferguson knew existed: they went round and round, in small circles and in big ones, and every so often Ivar grasped his hips and lifted him up and spun him round so he was completely untethered by

anything other than Ivar's hands, and in between the lifting and the spinning-round Ivar held him close and made
the fast and raucous music with his mouth, music that
was unlike anything John Ferguson had heard before, and
he wondered if Ivar was making it up as he went along –
if he was making the dance up too, or if they were both
things he was remembering from long ago. Ivar lifted
him up again and John Ferguson heard himself shout. He
tried not to but he did. It was thrilling to feel Ivar's hands
clamp him hard like that on his hips and then to be almost
thrown upwards with the air rushing into his body. Each
time it happened he heard himself shout again from the
shock and thrill of it. They knocked against the table and
against Ivar's great chair and against the bed, and the only
thought in John Ferguson's head was that he didn't want
it to stop, and when at last it did, and Ivar spun him to a
halt, John Ferguson was so breathless he couldn't speak.
His arms hung at his sides. He lowered his head and, to
his vast distress, he was crying.

'Forgive me,' he whispered, hardly knowing who he was
talking to, only knowing that he was guilty.

36

At first it was almost like in the beginning, when John Ferguson had been the patient and Ivar the nurse – John Ferguson lying quite still and trying to hold on to his stillness even though it was almost unbearable, taking shallow breaths while Ivar attended to his body, tentatively to start with, and then more confidently. But as Ivar became more confident, so did John Ferguson; he stopped trying to stifle his own noise, and although at first he'd wanted it to be dark, soon, like Ivar, he wanted the smoky illumination of the lamp too.

Ivar's skin was grimy, and smelled of smoke and fish, but he was paler than John Ferguson had expected him to be, and the parts of him he'd never seen before – his chest and his back, the tops of his arms, his legs and his buttocks, everywhere that wasn't habitually exposed to the elements – did not have the hardened, weather-worn feel of his face and forearms, and especially not of his hands, which were scarred and thickened on the palms and the tops, like hide.

There were places on his upper arms and round his hips where the skin was loose, and John Ferguson remembered Ivar telling him how the flesh had fallen off him this past winter because he'd been ill and hadn't eaten for a long time.

When they were finished Ivar tugged at a fold of skin under one of his arms and laughed. 'Look,' he said. 'I am old.'

To which John Ferguson responded by taking hold of the loose skin of his own arm, and laughed too, and said, 'So am I.'

There was no more light now from the lamp and the fire was almost out. They lay in front of the hearth with their faces turned towards each other. 'There is something I have to tell you,' said John Ferguson.

He'd been about to tell him before.

After the dancing he'd begun to speak, but he'd been crying then, and Ivar had put his hand over his mouth and hushed him, and after that there'd been no more talking until Ivar said, 'Look. I am old.'

Now Ivar was pulling the blanket round them both.

'There is—' John Ferguson began again, but Ivar stopped him, and said it was all right. He knew he'd come from the estate. He'd found his box in the Baillie house. He knew everything.

John Ferguson shook his head, and for a moment he closed his eyes.

'No,' he said. 'You don't. Not everything.'

37

There was a word in Ivar's language for the moment before something happens; for the state of being on the brink of something.

He'd tried several times to explain it using words John Ferguson already knew – with mimes and charades involving the water and the weather – but John Ferguson had never been able to grasp what it was he was trying to tell him.

In due course, John Ferguson will understand it.

In due course, after a fair amount of back-and-forth and to-ing and fro-ing, he will arrive at a precise and succinct definition of it – a definition in which he will give, as examples of the sort of moment it describes, 'the last moment before the tide turns; the last moment of day before night begins'.

It was still early when Ivar woke and got up to riddle the ash in the fireplace, push the remains of the peats into the centre and blow on them until they began to burn and slowly warm the place.

He sat then for a while in his great chair waiting for the fire to come back to life, watching John Ferguson breathe, and now and then shift his body.

*

When John Ferguson had finished telling him who he was and what was to happen, Ivar had asked him to tell him again, as if the news was so vast he hadn't been able fully to absorb it the first time.

After that they'd lain very still beneath the blanket and for a long time neither of them spoke, until in the end Ivar had whispered, 'I am afraid of the water,' and John Ferguson had said, 'So am I.'

38

Mary was awake most of the night and in the early hours the skipper, Mr Baxter, knocked softly on a board outside her berth and said, 'We are close now, Mrs Ferguson. I thought you would want to know.'

He could provide her with a swimming belt, he said, if she was anxious about the short stretch in the boat from the *Laura* to the shore. The men would wait while she fetched her husband and then they would be away again, and Trondheim was not a bad place to spend a few days before they turned round and returned to Kirkwall.

'Thank you, Mr Baxter. I am ready when you are.'

Which was true: Mary – as she'd been for almost the entire journey, almost from the time she left Penicuik and all the way on the *Velocity* from Leith to Kirkwall and then on the *Laura* from Kirkwall to Lerwick and from Lerwick to now – was up and dressed and ready and impatient.

39

The operation of the pistol was more complicated than he thought it would be – he turned it over in his hands, squeezing his eyes shut and trying to picture the calm and easy way Strachan had handled it while he sat outside the Baillie house: which pieces you had to open and close and which ones were supposed to move; where to put the powder, where the ammunition and the scrap of cotton.

He had no plan.

All that can be said is that preventing Strachan's men from landing was the only act he could think of that would stop everything coming to an end, and he latched on to it with a kind of mad faith.

On a clear day he would have seen that the vessel from which the boat had come was not the *Lily Rose* but something smaller, slighter, like an ordinary trading smack.

On a clear day he would have seen that the occupants of the boat were not who he expected them to be.

On a clear day he would have recognised Mary.

But the day was not clear, the white mist had thickened into a low-slung bluish fog that had tucked itself between the shore and the skerries, veiling them and the *Laura* and everything else beyond them, and falling in a cloudy haze over the shallow water close to the beach.

He had not expected it to be today. John Ferguson had said he thought they had a little more time – another week perhaps, a few days at least, depending on the weather and the tides.

40

It was difficult, keeping the *Laura* off the rocks as they drew near, and the four crew did what they could to fight against the current with her two enormous sweep oars. But after an hour they were no nearer the shore, and in the end Mary said she would go now in the boat if they'd take her, which is what happened – the skipper, Mr Baxter, being confident the little boat would manage all right because although there was a heavy swell, there were no broken waves.

It was only the suddenness and completeness of the mist he hadn't reckoned with, and watching from the *Laura*, he and Mr Lane quickly lost sight of the boat and saw nothing until after the sharp, mechanical explosion, when the sky turned black above the mist with thousands and thousands of birds: a sudden immense darkness, pulsing and thick, as if it had a billowing new lining.

41

From the house John Ferguson heard the tremendous crack, and out on the water, Mary's head snapped back.

For a moment she looked up at the sky, to see where the noise had come from, but there was only blackness and the crazy confusion of the birds, their shrieking, and, close by, the shouting and cursing of the oarsmen – the clouded world breaking open like a stage from which its heavy velvet curtain has been lifted – and she saw a strip of grey sand and dark rocks behind; cliffs and, high up, a fuzz of green, and the birds, still swooping and darting madly; a big, fair, bearded man up to his waist in the water not ten yards in front of her.

The men from the *Laura* were all shouting at once, the burliest of them leaping out of the boat and splashing through the shallows, loudly abusing the big man for shooting at them.

And then suddenly John was there, laying his hands gently on the man, taking the pistol from him and talking to him and touching his face with his palm.

Mary watched from the boat – the burly oarsman still shouting and looking as though he was trying to land a punch on the big man, and John trying to appease him, pointing up at the sky and gesticulating – explaining to him, Mary supposed, that the man had only been shooting at the birds.

The other three oarsmen stayed with Mary, holding on to the boat while it rocked on the water and was pushed towards the shore. She watched John walk the big man out of the sea on to the beach, and then he came wading back out to meet her, dragging his left leg as if he'd injured it since she'd last seen him. 'Mary!' he called out. 'Oh my goodness, Mary!'

It was as if the three of them had forgotten how to speak.

Ivar warmed a pan of milk and poured some into a bowl for her to drink.

Her skirt was wet almost up to her waist and drooped heavily on to the clay floor. She sat next to the fire in Ivar's big chair, and while she drank the warm milk steam rose into the smoky atmosphere from her dress.

She looked around at the two thick shelves, the one above the hearth and the one over the door. She looked at the big wicker chair and the various wooden boxes and at the stiff sheepskin bag in the corner, brimming with dirty-looking wool. She looked at the spinning wheel and the wooden bed and at John's satchel hanging from a peg in the wall; she looked at the pretty teapot on the shelf above the door and the knitted blankets on the floor and at the low table, which had John's writing tin on it, and the pistol, which he had carried back from the beach and set down next to a bowl of half-eaten porridge.

The men from the *Laura* would wait, they said, while she dried out a little and her husband packed his things.

John sat on the bed, holding her hand, eventually trying

to lighten the atmosphere by saying, 'That probably wasn't the welcome you were expecting.'

He was so sorry, he kept saying. It was Keane Ivar had wanted to shoot, not her.

'He is very upset. About having to leave.'

'Of course he is,' said Mary. She could hear how sharp her own voice sounded, how tight. 'Strachan knew he would be.' It was why she'd come all this way. The factor had known it all along. She'd been certain something terrible would happen and she had wanted to prevent it.

'Oh Mary.'

Ivar stood at the table in his wet trousers, cutting up a fish and dividing it between two plates, one for Mary and one for John, scraping the rest directly on to the table and eating it with his fingers as he worked.

John Ferguson's wife, though unmistakably the same person as the one in her picture, was smaller than he'd imagined. Most of her size, he saw now, came from the largeness of her clothes – her dress and her coat and the thick cape she wore over her shoulders. Her face, meanwhile, was without doubt the one in the portrait, except that it was keener in the flesh, less shy, and her gaze when she looked around herself was alert and searching.

He said something in his language to John Ferguson and John Ferguson replied.

'You speak his language now?' said Mary, amazed.

She sipped the milk. She touched the red knitted sleeve of his coat. 'What happened?'

'I fell – I tore it. Ivar mended it.'

She looked around again at the room – at the table and

the teapot and the wooden boxes and the bags of wool and the bed where, underneath, John's spare clothes – his shirt and his underwear – were neatly folded in a small pile with her picture on top in its leather frame, the glass a little cracked but otherwise intact.

She could never say how she knew, but she did.

It was in John and it was in the man.

She'd seen it on the beach, though she hadn't known it then. She hadn't known it on the walk up either, when John kept saying how sorry he was she'd had such a fright and how glad he was to see her and how much he'd missed her and how Ivar hadn't meant to hurt her in any way. But she knew it now, and with every second that passed while John sat holding her hand and Ivar stood bent over the fish, she wished that Keane would come, or, better still, that he was already here, standing over Ivar and watching him pack up his meagre possessions before removing him from their lives forever.

She wanted desperately to say something that established her connection to John – something that bound him to her, instead of to this big bearded man whose name was Ivar, but it was as if she was still stupefied by the shock of the explosion at the beach and she couldn't think of anything to say.

She put the bowl of milk on the floor and stood up. 'Would you excuse me, John, for a few minutes?'

And perhaps that was when John Ferguson knew that she knew, because he got up and went after her and at the door he said, 'Mary, I am so glad to see you.' Which was the truth, and even if it wasn't the whole truth it was the only one he was capable of expressing.

Mary paused. She put her hand on his arm. 'I know you are, John. I do know that.'

In the narrow space between Ivar's low-roofed house and the byre she stood for a few moments, and then she followed the wall at the bottom of the homefield until she came to the path they'd come up on from the beach and kept walking. She walked over stones and through puddles and reeds, and at the foot of a small rounded hill she sat down on a stone.

The mist had cleared completely and in the distance she could see the *Laura* at anchor beyond the skerries. She rolled the hem of her skirt in both her fists and squeezed it hard and watched the seawater run out on to the ground.

In Pitlochry once, when she was a girl, she had fallen in love with a Chinese spoon in the window of a shop.

Thinking that somehow she could beg enough money from her father to buy it, she'd gone in and asked to have a closer look, but when she saw the spoon being taken away from all the other bits and pieces around it in the window and carried by itself in the shopkeeper's hand, she knew she'd made a mistake. It came back to her, this small revelation, while she sat looking out across the heather and the black soil and the vast grey of the sea. It seemed too banal a story to repeat to John, but it was what she was thinking: that this would not have happened if he hadn't found himself in such unfamiliar surroundings, and as soon as he left them he would know that what had occurred had been an aberration.

She tugged at the grass around the stone and threw handfuls of it into the air and watched them break up and scatter and go tumbling off along the path in the wind.

Her life seemed to be separating itself into three different parts, each one with a beginning and an end.

First there'd been the time when she was growing up in Penicuik, which had contained her friendship with Alice Monk; then there'd been the years after Alice left, and her father died – when she'd been busy with her walks and her books and had been more or less alone but in no way unhappy; and then there'd been the third part – her time with John, which had arrived so unexpectedly and which, although it had been the shortest, had been the most important, and she wondered if what she was looking at now was the fourth and final part.

At the house she sat down on the bed, and when John reached for her hand she gave it to him.

Ivar was outside, talking to the black cow, and while she and John sat on the bed holding hands, they both looked at him through the open door. Mary thought he seemed older than John, but was perhaps younger. She watched him walking away from the cow. His clothes fluttered, pressing themselves against his shoulders and the backs of his legs, and she was sharply conscious that John's eyes followed him too as he moved up and down between the short rows of some crop she didn't recognise, picking up stones and pulling out weeds and looking like someone who still thought there was a chance he could go on like that forever; that even now he wouldn't have to give up everything he loved.

How is it, she thought, we never see the big things coming?

She watched him walk up towards the top of the field and thought of the Comrie earthquake; the extraction of her teeth.

Both had been terrible surprises, and yet they had led to great and unanticipated happiness.

She turned her eyes away from Ivar and looked at John. You never knew in advance if a decision was the right one. All you could do was try to imagine the future and use that to help you make up your mind in a difficult situation, and if you couldn't imagine the future, well, you had to make up your mind anyway.

'He could come with us,' she said. 'Instead of two, we could be three.'

42

Mr Baxter – after a lot of begging and the promise of the proceeds from the Wedgwood teapot, which they would sell when they got to Trondheim – agreed to bring Pegi.

It took an hour and a half to swim her out past the skerries and hoist her on board, and although she struggled against the ropes when they lifted her out of the water, and clipped Mr Lane, the linen merchant, painfully on his right elbow with her hoof as they swung her past him, that part of things went smoothly enough.

The sheep and the chickens and the old blind cow, it was decided, would have to take their chances when Keane arrived, and although this was not ideal, Ivar, like Mary, seemed to accept that their situation was complicated, and that this was the best they could do.

None of them spoke much to each other while all this was going on – neither John to Mary, nor Mary to John, nor either of the Fergusons to Ivar, nor Ivar to John or Mary; nothing beyond what was necessary for the gathering together of what was to be taken and its transportation to the *Laura*. It was as if all three were carrying inside themselves the delicate balance of what they were doing, and were afraid to disturb it in any way.

In time, Mary thought, she would ask John about his plans for the Church.

He'd made no mention of them while they were helping Ivar pack, and his departure from the old Church to the new one seemed a long time ago now, as if the new one itself was already old. But he would talk to her about it all when he was ready, she knew him well enough for that, just as she knew it was in the nature of Churches to be constantly splintering, and dividing, and disagreeing about things, and starting again. It was their speciality, she supposed, and she would have to wait and see what, if anything, he came up with.

Meanwhile it was very cramped in their makeshift quarters on the *Laura*, and when they weren't up on deck they were crushed together on the floor, and although John seemed preoccupied at times, he was mostly busy, with Ivar, showing Mary the pile of papers on which were written all the words they had so far recorded, and which Ivar spoke aloud to Mary so she would know them too.

As the need arose, they added new ones – words for sail and eider-duck, for seasickness and toothache, and other more difficult, less tangible notions, like *snipr* – something rolled up or entangled, or *skrim* – a glimpse, a faint shining. They added the word for 'husband' and the word for 'wife', and when John Ferguson ran out of ink he borrowed a small bottle of iodine from Mr Baxter's medicine box so they could keep going, and although the words were a little pale on the page they were legible, and like a prayer, or a gentle weather forecast, they accompanied Ivar and the Fergusons on their journey north.

Author's Note

The story I have imagined in *Clear* takes place in 1843, the year of the Great Disruption in the Scottish Church, when 474 ministers (roughly one third of the total number) rebelled against the system of patronage, whereby Scotland's landowners had the power to install ministers of their choice in parishes on their estates. These rebellious ministers broke away to form the new Free Church, giving up their manses and their churches to start again from scratch.

These are the circumstances in which my own John Ferguson finds himself – circumstances which bring him up against another of Scotland's great historic social upheavals: the Clearances, which began in the Lowlands in the mid eighteenth century and continued into the second half of the nineteenth in the Highlands and Islands. Whole communities of the rural poor were forcibly removed from their homes by landowners in a relentless programme of coercive and systematic dispossession to make way for crops, cattle and – increasingly as time went on – sheep.

In the final stages of the Clearances, the consequences (still visible today in the ruins and decaying stone remains littering parts of the landscape) were truly catastrophic for an entire swathe of Scottish society that was no longer wanted. Landlords did everything in their power – and their power was absolute – to empty out the land in pursuit of profit. Many families were moved on to plots of marginal ground deliberately designed to be too small to support them. Compelled to seek additional work elsewhere in order to survive, they became a source of temporary and seasonal labour that landlords could call on when it suited them. Meanwhile the newly displaced crofters did the best they could with the land they'd been moved to by planting potatoes, and when the potato blight arrived in 1846, they began to starve.

Thousands upon thousands, between 1750 and 1860, were evicted, or driven by famine to leave their homes. Some made their way to the big industrialised cities in the south of Scotland; others – either on their own account or as part of organised expatriation schemes – sought passage to the United States, Canada and Australia in search of a new life.

For Ivar's language, I have drawn on Jakob Jakobsen's *Etymological Dictionary of the Norn Language in Shetland* (first published in Danish, in four volumes, between 1908 and 1921). Now extinct, Norn was once spoken on the islands of Orkney and Shetland in the far north of Scotland, but began to die out after the Danish king pawned the islands to Scotland in 1469. Gradually, Norn was replaced by a dialect of Scots and, while its ghostly influence can still be felt today in the survival of certain words, it had all but disappeared by the time Jakobsen did his research. Its last known native speaker is said to have been Walter Sutherland, who died in 1850, on Unst, the most northerly of the Shetland Isles, though it may have lingered a little longer on the most remote, Foula.

The island Ivar inhabits won't be found on any map; in my imagination its location is between Shetland and Norway, and in this faraway spot his dialect has stayed close to its Norn origins – a distinctive tongue which, by the time John Ferguson meets him, is well on its way to disappearing.

The meanings of the words used by John Ferguson on pages 72, 78, 88, 120 and 123 are listed below in order of appearance:

gilgal	uproar in the sea
skreul	commotion in the sea with heavy breakers, especially the sound of it surging around sunken rocks
pulter	crested or cross-sea
yog	heavy sea with short, choppy waves
fester	uproar in the sea, especially at a change in the wind
dreetslengi	high, running sea
o	stream
gruggy	dark and threatening (of weather)
bunki	round wooden tub for storing lamp oil
greut	dregs of lamp oil
flinter	to bustle about
flogs	tufts
snyag	thin wool
skerpin	wind-dried coalfish

snori	violet (the flower)
for	ditch
flodreks	limpets
flingaso	water in which limpets have been scalded
tur	faint firelight
gob	puddle; swampy spot
gagl	moist, soft mass
degi	swamp; morass; very wet ground
dyapl	slush; mire
dwog	small puddle; dirty place
diun	swamp; marshy hollow
skump	fog bank; thick haze
gyolm	dense fog
blura	dense bluish fog along the shore in calm weather, a harbinger of wind
ask	bank of fog
dunk	haze; drizzle; damp fog
syora	very dense black mist lying on the surface of the sea
mirkabrod	misty clouds drifting before the wind
groma	light mist, especially with rifts through which blue sky is seen
rag	thick, damp mist
nombrastom	very thick mist
dalareek	mist rising from low-lying stagnant water
himna	slight covering of mist along the shore
yema	mist lying on the surface of the water
dom	slight mist in fine, warm weather
ga	low, threatening, storm-charged cloud

glob	detached, dark rain cloud
homek	big, heavy, snow-laden cloud
benker	heavy cloud ascending on the horizon
elin	dark cloud in frosty weather
glodrek	big, dark cloud with a whitish top through which the sun shines
binder	cold north-easterly wind that makes the earth hard and dry
gas	cold northerly wind
asel	cold, keen wind
geul	faint breeze; gentle, steady wind
snaver	a piece of wood between the strands of a tether to prevent it from twisting
hoss	muffled murmur; sound of waves lapping the shore in calm weather
horl	distant rolling sound of the sea
yal	shriek, cry, especially of gulls
tusk	rustle
snirk	creak

Note: The Norn spellings are John Ferguson's. In Jakobsen's dictionary, *diun* appears as *dien*; *dreetslengi* as *drittslengi*; *dyapl* as *djapl*; *geul* as *gøl*; *gyolm* as *gjolm*; *greut* as *grøt*; *leura* as *lørra*; *liki* as *likki*; *skreul* as *skrøl*; *snyag* as *snjag*; *syora* as *sjara*; *yal* as *jal*; *yog* as *jogg*. Please also note that I've used 'corn' to mean 'oats', in keeping with contemporary usage and David Nutt's two-volume English translation of Jakobsen's dictionary (1928 and 1932).

Acknowledgements

Above all, I'm indebted to the indefatigable Jakob Jakobsen, whose extraordinary dictionary I stumbled across late one winter's afternoon in the Reading Room at the National Library of Scotland in Edinburgh. This story grew out of the thousands of words he collected, and I would never have written it without them.

I'm also grateful to the Aberdeen Art Gallery, the Kelvingrove Museum, the Orkney Museum, the National Library of Scotland, the National Museum of Scotland, the New York Public Library and the Scottish National Portrait Gallery for all the books, manuscripts, letters, paintings and other treasures which have captured my imagination over the years.

Thank you to Richard Jenkins on Orkney, for talking to me about sheep.

Thank you to James Temple of Stowe, also on Orkney, and to Rob and Sue Gore-Langton for their kindness and help.

Thank you to Joshua Hillis.

Thank you to Chloe Briggs at the Free Presbytery Hall in Edinburgh for arranging for me to see David Octavius Hill's painting, *The First General Assembly of the Free*

Church of Scotland, Signing the Act of Separation and Deed of Demission.

Thank you to Seren Adams, Marion Duvert, Lamorna Elmer, Linden Lawson, Christine Lo, Pru Rowlandson and everyone at Granta, Scribner, The Clegg Agency and United Agents who worked on the book. To Bill Clegg, boundless gratitude for his imaginative care and invaluable insights in his early readings of the manuscript. Very special thanks also to Nan Graham, Sally Howe, Bella Lacey and Anna Webber.

To Michael, as ever and always, thank you.

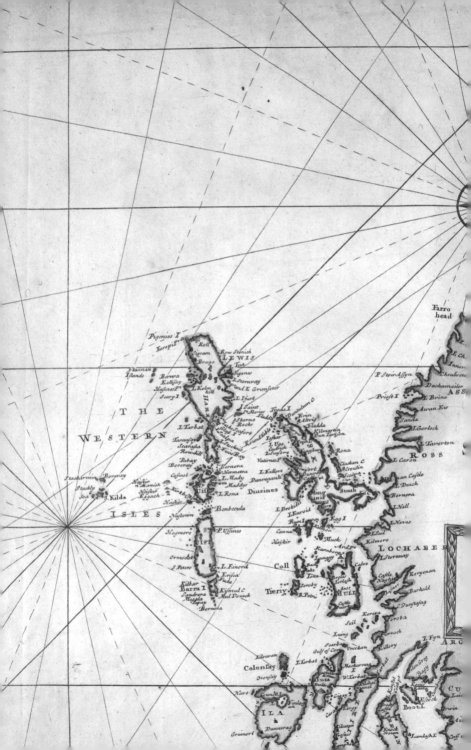